Refugee Boy

Refugee Boy

Benjamin Zephaniah

BLOOMSBURY
CHILDREN'S
BOOKS

- W I T H   T H A N K S -

To Dr. David Appleyard for his assistance with
the Amharic dialect

Copyright (c) 2001 by Benjamim Zephaniah

Published by Bloomsbury, New York and London
Distributed to the trade by St. Martin's Press
Library of Congress Cataloging-in-Publication Data
available upon request.
LC: 2001043970
ISBN:1-58234-763-8
First U.S. Edition
1 3 5 7 9 10 8 6 4 2
Printed in Great Britain

Bloomsbury USA Children's Books
175 Fifth Avenue
New York, New York 10010

For Million and Dereje Hailemariam

~ *Ethiopia* ~

As the family lay sleeping, soldiers kicked down the door of the house and entered, waving their rifles around erratically and shouting at the top of their voices. Alem ran into the room where his parents were, to find that they had been dragged out of bed dressed only in their nightclothes, and forced to stand facing the wall.

The soldier who was in command went and stood so that his mouth was six inches away from Alem's father's ear and shouted, 'What kind of man are you?'

Alem's father shuddered with fear; his voice trembled as he replied, 'I am an African.'

Alem looked on terrified as the soldier shot a number of bullets into the floor around the feet of his father and mother.

His mother screamed with fear. 'Please leave us! We only want peace.'

The soldier continued shouting. 'Are you Ethiopian or Eritrean? Tell us, we want to know.'

'I am an African,' Alem's father replied.

The soldier raised his rifle and pointed it at Alem's

father. 'You are a traitor.' He turned and pointed the rifle at Alem's mother. 'And she is the enemy.' Then he turned and pointed the rifle at Alem's forehead. 'And he is a mongrel.'

Turning back to Alem's father, he dropped his voice and said, 'Leave Ethiopia or die.'

~ *Eritrea* ~

As the family lay sleeping, soldiers kicked down the door of the house and entered, waving their rifles around erratically and shouting at the top of their voices. Alem ran into the room where his parents were, to find that they had been dragged out of bed dressed only in their nightclothes, and forced to stand facing the wall.

The soldier who was in command went and stood so that his mouth was six inches away from Alem's mother's ear and shouted, 'What kind of woman are you?'

Alem's mother shuddered with fear; her voice trembled as she replied, 'I am an African.'

Alem looked on terrified as the soldier shot a number of bullets into the floor around the feet of his mother and father.

His father screamed with fear. 'Please leave us! We only want peace.'

The soldier continued shouting. 'Are you Eritrean or Ethiopian? Tell us, we want to know.'

'I am an African,' Alem's mother replied.

The soldier raised his rifle and pointed it at Alem's mother. 'You are a traitor.' He turned and pointed the rifle at Alem's father. 'And he is the enemy.' Then he turned and pointed the rifle at Alem's forehead. 'And he is a mongrel.'

Turning back to Alem's mother, he dropped his voice and said, 'Leave Eritrea or die.'

CHAPTER 1

~ Welcome to the Weather ~

'Welcome to England, Mr Kelo,' said the immigration officer as he handed back the passports to Alem's father.

Alem stared up at the tall officer; the officer looked down at Alem. 'Have a good holiday now.'

'Thank you,' said Alem's father. He took Alem's hand and began to head for the baggage-reclaim area.

Alem jerked his father's hand and stopped suddenly. 'Abbaye, yaw teguru tekatlowal,' he said, brimming with excitement.

His father turned to him and spoke as if he was trying to shout quietly. 'What did I tell you? From now on you must try to speak English, you must practise your English – all right, young man?'

Alem panicked. 'Ishi abbaye,' he said.

His father's response was swift. 'English, I said.'

'Yes, Father.'

'Now what did you say?'

Alem looked back towards passport control. 'Father, that man who looked at the passports, what was wrong with him?'

11

'He looked all right to me.'

'I think something was wrong with his hair, he looked burned. Did you see his hair? It was red, red like sunset, he looked hot, he looked burned.'

His father shook his head and they continued to walk. 'No, nothing is wrong with him. This type of hair is called ginger. In England you will see many people with this colour hair – and you must not say burned, you must say burnt – the word is "burnt".'

As they stood waiting for their luggage to appear on the carousel, Alem looked up at the high ceiling. He loved the large airport building, it reminded him of space stations that he had seen in science-fiction films. Everything seemed so busy but so organised; everything looked so large. He looked towards the next carousel, where people were waiting for their luggage after a flight from India. Many of the people were Sikhs; the men were wearing turbans. They looked familiar. 'Father, are they all priests?' Alem asked.

'They are from India,' his father replied, 'they are called Sikhs. Just like our priests they wear turbans, and they are also religious, but I have never seen any in Ethiopia.'

They collected their luggage and headed towards the exit. Alem was looking around frantically, trying to take in the big building and all the different people while trying to avoid bumping into anyone, which he inevitably did a couple of times before reaching the customs hall.

The customs hall had an eerie atmosphere about it; customs officers stood silently observing as the passengers passed through in a rather nervous silence. The silence was broken by a large bearded officer leaning over his counter in the direction of Alem and his father. 'Excuse me, sir, could I have a word with you, please?'

'Certainly,' replied Alem's father as politely as he could.

'Could you put your luggage on the table, please, sir?'

As the officer spoke, he was looking behind and in front of the couple. 'Just the two of you travelling, sir?'

'Yes,' Alem's father replied, looking behind to make sure they had not attracted any followers.

'Now this is just a routine check, sir. I just need to ask you a few questions and provided everything is all right, you should be on your way soon. Right, sir, where have you arrived from?'

'Addis Ababa, Ethiopia.'

'Did you pack your suitcases yourself?'

'Yes.'

'What is the purpose of your visit?'

'We are having a holiday.'

'I take it this is your son?'

'Yes.'

'Could you tell me why you only have two pieces of luggage? It does seem odd,' said the customs officer as he looked around their feet for other pieces.

'Well, we only have one each because we are only going to be staying for a short time and we were planning to buy many things here in London, in the famous Oxford Road and Piccadilly Circle,' Alem's father replied, trying to put on the best upper-class accent that he could, but sounding rather clumsy.

'I think you mean Oxford Street and Piccadilly Circus. Could I see your passports, please?'

The man spent a good two minutes checking the passports before he put them down on the table next to the suitcases. Alem could sense that the words the customs officer was speaking were well rehearsed, he could sense that he was trying to be well-mannered and inoffensive, but at the same time there was something dangerous about him. It was as if he were an animal of prey waiting for a chance to pounce.

'So you are having a short holiday, sir? I would have thought that after coming all this way you would want to stay with us a little bit longer. Do you mind if I have a look in the cases, sir?'

'No, not at all. You should do what you have to do.'

The officer spent the next five minutes searching through the luggage. Alem wanted to tell him to be careful when he started to search his case but he was very self-conscious of the fact that his English wasn't great. In fact, Alem's English was quite good but he had never spoken English to an English person before. So he just watched in silence as the officer looked inside his schoolbooks and his toiletry bag, he even checked his underpants and looked in his socks. The officer then made an attempt to pack everything back as he had found it but it wasn't happening. Alem's father ended up helping him to push everything into the cases as best they could before the officer gave them permission to continue.

'That will be all, sir. I'm sorry for keeping you and I thank you for your co-operation.'

By now Alem's father was so annoyed that he didn't respond, he just picked up the suitcases and the passports and they continued towards the exit.

After changing some traveller's cheques, they headed outside for a taxi. It was a damp and chilly October day, and the sky over Heathrow was grey.

'It will rain, Father,' said Alem as he pointed to the sky.

His father smiled. 'You haven't been here for one hour yet but you have become English already; the English always talk about the weather. No, young man, that is not rain clouds, that is just English clouds. You will get used to them, they come with the territory.'

They approached a waiting taxi and Alem's father

15

handed a card to the driver. 'Is that where you wanna go, mate?' he asked, holding the card away from himself to compensate for his long-sightedness.

Alem's father nodded. 'Yes, please.'

'The Palace Hotel, High Street, Datchet, Berkshire. That's just up the road. I don't go there often – good job too, I'd never earn a living. OK, hop in.'

They did and they were on their way.

Alem's father came from the Amhara tribe of Ethiopia. His large forehead, light-brown skin and large eyes were typical of his people, as was his short, jet-black, curly hair. It is said that the Amhara people have Arab as well as African blood flowing through their veins, and the facial features of Alem and his father did reinforce that theory. He was a man who tried to smile as much as he could to please others but he took the business of life very seriously. In the taxi he sat straight-backed throughout the journey and looked silently straight ahead while Alem's eyes explored the black taxi's interior. Even the back of the taxi was a source of wonder for Alem, but his excitement was contained as he could see that his father wasn't in the mood. He looked deep in thought. To keep his mind occupied Alem tried to practise his English by reading the notices in the cab, whispering the words as he read them: 'No smok-ing. Li-censed

Hack-ney Car-riage. Red light in-di-cates doors are locked. This seat-belt is for your per-son-al safe-ty.'

After a while his attention turned to the road out-side, the M4. It was so straight and wide; the ride was so smooth, no potholes, no wild bends, just the sound of the engine and the tyres on the road.

They had travelled for only about seven miles when they turned off the motorway and headed towards the village down Majors Farm Road. It sud-denly went quiet; there were very few cars on the road and no farms to be seen, just a few empty fields. As they neared the village, Alem looked towards all the semi-detached houses for any sign of life. He could see the houses but where were the people? All the houses had cars in their driveways, usually two, and many had cats in the windows, but no people. He looked up at the chimneys and wondered what they were there for.

When they entered the village, things became a little busier but still remained very orderly. And now Alem began to see animals; they were only dogs that people had on leads but he was sure that he would soon see the local goats and chickens.

The taxi pulled up outside the hotel. It was an old-fashioned building that looked to Alem more like a big house than a hotel, after all, he had seen the Holiday Inn in Addis Ababa and he thought that was a big skyscraper, so he expected English hotels to be even bigger.

'Here you are, guvs,' said the driver, 'the Palace Hotel, wot a lavely little 'ous.'

Alem and his father couldn't understand what he said, but they knew that they had arrived.

'I beg your pardon?' By now Alem's father had dropped his pseudo-posh accent.

The taxi driver pointed to the house and spoke louder and slower. 'That is a love-er-ly little house, I said.'

'Oh, yes,' replied Alem's father as he raised the corners of his lips a tiny little bit in order to represent a smile. 'It is a nice building. How much money shall I pay you?'

'Eighteen quid and fifty pee, boss.'

It was a family-run three-star hotel with a pub and restaurant. The walls of the reception area were covered with paintings of idyllic English countryside scenes that led all the way up the oak stairs. Alem and his father stood at the desk for a few minutes waiting for someone to come. After checking out all the paintings and reading all the notices, Alem's father rang the miniature brass bell that was on the reception counter. Immediately a man appeared from the room behind the counter, a very big, bearded man who Alem thought looked very much like the customs officer they had not long left, except this man had a smile and no uniform.

'What can I do for you, sir?' he said, towering above both of them.

'We have a twin room reserved for us. My name is Mr Kelo, I spoke to you on the phone last week.'

The big man flicked through the pages of the registration book on the desk until he found the right page. 'Oh yes, that's right, Mr Kelo, a twin room for four nights for you and your son,' he said. Alem struggled to understand his accent. 'Did you have a pleasant flight?'

'Yes; it was a little crowded and we didn't get much sleep, but it was quite pleasant.'

'Well, we have given you a room in a very quiet part of the hotel where you can sleep for as long as you like. Even the trains are quiet here. Follow me, I'll take you there.'

As they walked upstairs to the room, the man kept talking. 'Only four nights with us?'

'I'm afraid so,' said Alem's father, following behind him.

'You'll need more than four days.'

'Four days is all we have,' Alem's father said abruptly.

The big man stopped suddenly, forcing Alem and his father to stop suddenly behind him. 'I'm just trying to be friendly, sir.'

Alem's father looked hesitantly towards Alem, then

towards the big man. 'I'm sorry, sir, I'm a bit tired, I think I need some sleep. My apologies. Actually we weren't sure how long we were going to be staying in the area. I have been told that there are many interesting places to see in England so we may move around a little.'

'Oh yes, there certainly is much to see,' said the man, continuing up the stairs. 'It's not just England, you know – if you get the chance you should visit Scotland. I've lived down here for most of my life but I was born in bonnie Scotland. When I want a holiday, where do I go? Scotland, of course. I've never forgotten my roots.'

The room was medium-sized and spotless. As the big man was telling his father about checkout and breakfast times, Alem headed straight for the window to see what kind of view they had. Sadly it was just the hotel car park and the backs of some other buildings, and if he put his head right up to the window and moved his eyeballs as far right as they could go, he could just about see a train station.

They spent the evening in the hotel room. Alem's father was much quieter than usual and spent most of his time reading a London guidebook while Alem watched television. It was Saturday night and most of the television channels were transmitting game shows or dating shows. Alem thought it was all very bizarre.

He was trying his best to understand what was being said but most of the time he just couldn't keep up with the pace of people's speech. From the moment that he landed he noticed that the English that he was hearing was very different from the English he had been taught at school. The customs officer had sounded different from the taxi driver and on the television everyone seemed to have his or her own accent. When Alem couldn't take it any longer, he switched off the television and went to look out of the window again. Nothing had changed, except it was now dark. He turned to his father. 'Nege, mindinnow yemminniseraw?'

'English,' his father replied abruptly, 'speak English.'

'I'm sorry, Father,' Alem continued. 'What will we do tomorrow, Father?'

'The holiday really starts tomorrow, young man. We will get a train into London and you will see all those famous places that you have seen in the books.'

And so it was. The next day they got a bus from Datchet to Reading and then a train from Reading into central London. In central London they boarded a sightseeing bus that took them to all the places they had seen in the books: Marble Arch, Piccadilly Circus, Buckingham Palace, Trafalgar Square, the Houses of Parliament and the Tower of London. Back home

Alem had lived only in small cities or towns and although he had been to the Ethiopian capital, he had never seen anything like London. Cities back home were busy with cars racing everywhere, but here it was so busy that the cars were standing still in traffic jams most of the time. The fumes emitted by the cars made Alem cough, he wondered why everyone else wasn't coughing until he got used to it and stopped.

When Alem was small he would always say that he wanted to make buildings when he grew up. Now he was sophisticated enough to say that he wanted to be an architect, so the buildings in London really caught his imagination. What he really liked about the city was the way the old and the new stood side by side. He thought this was also true of some parts of Ethiopia. He had seen places like the ancient obelisks at Axum and the churches carved out of the mountains at Lalibela. He always thought that if he became an architect he would try to bring the old and the new together, he would try to put old features into modern buildings.

He spent the whole day imagining how he would change London if he had the chance, and working out what bits of London he would take back home if he could.

After a visit to the British Museum they wandered

down Charing Cross Road and found themselves in Leicester Square. Alem's father wasn't sure where to go. Darkness began to descend and the people around them looked younger. Alem's father gave him a choice; they could go back to Datchet straight away or stay in London to eat and return later. Alem decided to stay in central London.

'So what do you want to eat?' Alem's father asked, looking rather devious. 'In London you can eat anything, the choice is yours.' He opened the guidebook he was clutching. 'Not far from where we are standing there is French food, Indian food, Chinese food, Mexican, Spanish, Italian –'

'Italian,' Alem interrupted quickly. 'Italian food, they have Italian food here?'

'Yes, of course,' came the reply. 'Don't forget we are in Europe and Italy is not that far from here – so you want Italian?'

'Yes please, spaghetti, please!' Alem was jumping with excitement.

Spaghetti was one of Alem's favourite foods. The Italian army invaded Eritrea in 1882, and then in 1935 they entered Ethiopia. Unable to conquer the country, they were soon chased out, but they left behind tanks, unexploded bombs and spaghetti. It wasn't the kind of food that was cooked in the house but sometimes Alem had spaghetti at school or on special occasions in restaurants.

Alem's father checked his map and as they headed for Covent Garden, he began to question Alem. 'So, Mr Spaghetti Lover, do you know where spaghetti comes from?'

'Easy,' Alem replied confidently. 'Italy.'

'That is where it originated but where does the spaghetti we eat back home actually come from?'

'Italy.' Alem insisted.

'No, that's not so true.'

'Of course it comes from Italy. You told me that spaghetti comes from Italy, Father.'

'Well, the truth is that most of the spaghetti we eat back home is made back home, but the spaghetti that we get here will be the real spaghetti, spaghetti from Italy.'

'Are you sure?'

'I am very sure. I know these things, you know,' Alem's father replied jokingly. 'Spaghetti back home tastes African, spaghetti here will taste Italian, you wait and see.'

But Alem had a comeback. 'You may know that spaghetti back home is made back home, but how can you be sure that spaghetti here is not made here? Maybe every country makes its own spaghetti.'

His father was genuinely stuck. 'Well, now – you have got me there. You have a point.' He paused for a moment before letting his alternative theory be known. 'Well, OK, the spaghetti you get in England may be made in England – but,' he said, raising a finger in the air, 'I bet that even the spaghetti that is made in England is made by Italians.'

Alem looked up at his father and raised an eyebrow, signifying that he was not so sure about his theory. Just then they found what was advertised in the guidebook as a genuine Italian restaurant, and there they ate spaghetti. Both agreed that the spaghetti tasted better than the spaghetti they got back home, but because neither of them could pluck up the courage to ask a waiter, the country of origin of the spaghetti was still unknown to them.

Soon they found themselves hurrying by Underground to Paddington station, where they managed to get the last train to Reading and from there the last bus to Datchet. The rush home seemed desperate but Alem loved the excitement of being out so late.

As the village clock struck midnight, they were just getting into bed. Alem was now reading the London guidebook while his father lay staring at the ceiling in deep contemplation.

Alem stopped reading and looked at his father. 'Father, can you hear that?' he said, turning his ear towards the window.

There was no response from his father.

'Father, can you hear that?'

Alem had caught his attention. 'I'm sorry, hear what?'

'Can you hear the nothing, Father? There are no animal noises – no birds, no donkeys, no hyenas, nothing.' As he finished speaking, a car roared through the streets.

'I don't think they have so many wild animals here, only wild drivers in loud cars,' his father replied as he sat up and looked towards Alem, whose bed was on the other side of the room. 'Did you have a good day, young man?'

'Yes, it was very good, Father. I liked all the buildings and the museum and I like also the food.'

'You should not say "I like also", you should say, "I also liked the food".'

'Yes, Father, I also liked the food,' Alem said, concentrating hard on his word order. 'Mother would like it too,' he continued, 'don't you think so, Father?'

'Yes, of course.' He got out of bed and crossed the room to sit on Alem's bed.

'What's the matter, Father?' Alem asked.

'Nothing,' he replied, sounding very serious. 'I just want you to know that your mother and I love you, son, and you know that anything we do is for the best. I have never been here but I know that England is a nice country, there are some good people here, you must remember that. And back home there are some good people too, not everyone back there wants to fight the war, most people would love to just get on with their lives. So remember, there are good and bad everywhere and your mother and I have always tried to do the best for you because we want you to be one of the good ones. Not a brave African warrior, not a powerful man or a rich man or a great hunter, we just want you to be a good person. Always remember that.' He leaned down and kissed Alem on his forehead, then made his way back to his own bed.

'Father, is something wrong?'

'No, young man, I just want you to try and be a good person,' he said, turning off the light. 'Good night – Dehinaider.'

'Good night, Father – Dehinaider, abba,' Alem replied.

CHAPTER 2

~ Alone in the Country ~

After a long, peaceful sleep, Alem woke up late the next morning to the sound of people moving in the hallway outside. For a moment he forgot where he was. For the second time in his life he was waking up outside Africa, to the strange smell of full English breakfasts being cooked below. He looked quickly to his father's bed but his father wasn't there. He presumed that his father had gone to arrange breakfast and he wanted to surprise him by being wide awake when he returned. He jumped out of bed and headed straight for the bathroom, where he showered as quickly as he could. Soon his hair was combed and he was dressed, waiting for his father.

After sitting silently for ten minutes, he turned the television on. The news was on and he watched in amazement as the newsreader told of how a baby had been stolen from its mother in a shop, and of how a homeless man was beaten as he lay sleeping in a doorway in the West End. Before ending the programme, the newsreader smiled and said, 'And finally on a lighter note. The people of Tower Hamlets were the happiest people in the land this morning when the Queen visited a local factory to thank the workers for their service to the community.' Alem watched as the workers waited in line for the Queen to greet them. He watched their faces, wondering if these were really the happiest people in the land; he wondered whether the Queen would also visit the homeless man that had been beaten when she was returning to the palace. He knew that the palace was not far from the West End.

There was a knock on the door. Alem turned the television off with the remote control. 'Hello,' he said curiously.

'Hello,' came the reply, 'it's Mr Hardwick, the hotel manager. Can I come in and have a word?'

'I don't think you can come in now,' Alem said nervously. 'My father is not here, but he will be back soon. I think he has gone for food.'

Ignoring this, Mr Hardwick opened the door to see Alem sitting on the bed. 'I need to speak to you,' he said solemnly as he entered the room. He went and sat down on a chair and continued to speak. 'Did you hear your father get up early this morning? It could have been while it was still dark – in the very early hours of the morning?'

'No,' Alem replied.

'This is a tough one, lad, I don't know how to say this but it seems that he did leave the hotel early this morning and he's left us all in a very awkward position.'

Alem was very puzzled. 'Awkward position?'

'Yes, he left two letters, one for me and one for you,' the manager said, reaching out and handing Alem a letter still sealed in its envelope. Alem opened it. It contained a photograph of Alem with his mother and father, and a handwritten letter. Alem read it silently as Mr Hardwick looked on.

My dearest son,

You have seen all the trouble that we have been going through back home. What is happening back there has nothing to do with us but we are stuck in the middle of it. You are the product of two countries, Ethiopia and Eritrea, and we love them both equally but they are pulling themselves and each other apart. We hope that it does not go on like this much longer but until the fighting stops and our persecution is over, your mother and I think that it would be best if you stay in England. Here they have organisations that will help you, compassionate people who understand why people have to seek refuge from war. We just cannot afford to risk another attack on you; we value your life more than anything.

Your mother and I will try to use our organisation to help bring about peace but if we fail and we see no hope, then we may be joining you soon. If things get better, you will be joining us soon, but you must understand that we don't want to see you suffer any more, and we don't want you to go through what we have been through.

We shall be writing to you soon, young man. Be strong, learn more English, and remember to love your neighbours because peace is better than war, wherever you live.
Your loving father

Alem held the letter and photo with both his hands on his lap and looked down in silence. Mr Hardwick looked around the room nervously, not sure how he should react. Then for a long moment they looked at each other before Mr Hardwick spoke. 'I have to say, lad, this has never happened here before and I'm not sure what to do. As far as I'm concerned you can stay here for two more nights, your father has paid for your room and all your meals, but you can't stay here for ever.' He looked down at the letter in Alem's hand, then at Alem himself, and spoke as if pleading. 'Your father says you have no family here – is this true? Don't you know anyone at all in England? Don't you have any friends here?'

Alem didn't speak; he just shook his head to every question.

'OK, well, the first thing we can do is to get you some breakfast,' Mr Hardwick said with a sigh of resignation.

Alem's breakfast was brought to his room that morning but his other meals were taken in the dining room with the other hotel guests. He always sat alone by the window, looking out at the little pond and watching the birds that would come to feed from the bird table.

That day Alem went for a short walk, which took him around the small grounds of Datchet, the parish church of St Mary the Virgin and the town centre. The town was as pretty as a postcard. At its centre on grassland between two roads he came upon a stone monument. He stood there to read the inscription, ignoring the cold wind that was making his eyes water. It had been erected by the inhabitants of Datchet to commemorate the Great War of 1914 to 1918. It spoke of the glorious forces and their allies by sea, on land and in the air who had fought against the combined forces of Germany, Austria, Turkey and Bulgaria. The monument simply reminded Alem of war. Nobody is glorious in war, he thought as he walked away to admire other more postive items from the past in an antique shop across the road.

Back at the hotel, Alem sat for a while in the garden and then went to his room to watch television and read the guidebook. The staff and guests at the hotel seemed friendly enough and he was keen to know why Mr Hardwick called him 'lad' but he didn't have the nerve to ask. He would exchange a few words with people at mealtimes but apart from that he spoke very little, which made the day seem very long. Trying to learn as much as he could about

British culture from the television meant that his mind was kept occupied, but every time there was silence he began to think about how he had got where he was. When did his parents have these conversations where they decided to bring him to England? Was bringing him to England really the best thing to do? Did they really love him or was this a plan to get rid of him? Would they care so much about his upbringing, his health, his education and then dump him?

At one point Alem even began to believe that this was some kind of rite-of-passage thing, a test of manhood, an initiation test to see how he would cope with being alone and having to fend for himself. As he walked down the different hallways in the hotel, he began to try and peep into the other rooms to see if his father was hiding in one of them.

The next morning after breakfast Alem walked down the two miles of country roads to Windsor. He had read about the castle and thought that he might be able to see it, but when he reached the edge of the town he turned around and went back to the hotel. He was worried that he might lose his way in what looked from the outskirts like a much bigger town.

Back in his hotel room he sat on his bed watching middle-aged women having makeovers on breakfast television when there was a knock on the door. Alem recognised the voice of Mr Hardwick.

'All right, lad? Can we come in? I'm with a couple of nice young ladies who would like to have a word with you.'

He entered the room, followed by two women who both immediately locked their eyes on Alem.

'This is the lad,' Mr Hardwick said, looking at one of the women. 'Alem's been a wonderful lad, everybody likes him, no trouble at all – I wish there were more like him.'

Alem felt slightly uncomfortable. Everybody's eyes were upon him, which made him feel a bit like an animal in a zoo. But when the woman spoke he felt different, much better.

'Tena-yestelen, Alem.'

'Tena-yestelen,' Alem replied.

'Ingilizinya tinnaggeralleh?' she asked.

'Yes, I speak English,' Alem said as he breathed a sigh of relief.

She was Ethiopian, she looked like someone from the Oromo tribe, dark, round-faced and slim. But what did she want? Alem wondered. Was she a good guy or a bad guy?

'My name is Mariam and this is Pamela. We come from an organisation called the Refugee Council. We heard that you were here and we have come to help you.'

Pamela was the taller of the two, white-skinned

with cheeks highlighted with red blusher and short jet-black hair. Alem knew very little about the tribes of England but he was curious about the tribe that Pamela belonged to. He had never seen a European with a silver stud in her chin and six earrings hanging from each ear before. Still she spoke plain English.

'First of all we need to know that you're OK, and then – well, then we have to try and do whatever you need. We are here for you.'

'I think I'll go now,' Mr Hardwick said, turning and heading for the door. 'You three take your time now. I'm downstairs if you need me.'

The moment Mr Hardwick left the room, the atmosphere changed. Mariam and Pamela sat on the two available chairs and Alem turned the television off with the remote control, which was still in his hand. Mariam's eyes wandered around the room and took in the photo of Alem with his parents, which was propped against the bedside lamp next to his bed. 'So what is it like here then?'

Alem leaned back and rested on his elbows, now feeling more at ease. 'It's OK. The people are nice but the food is very strange.'

'What do you find strange about the food?' Pamela asked.

'Well, it's not too bad but it's very dry. I don't understand why they made the food so dry, and then they gave me something called gravy to make the food more wet.'

Mariam and Pamela laughed out loud. Alem smiled with them. Pamela hadn't stopped laughing when she began speaking. 'You see, this is meat-and-two-veg territory.'

Alem repeated puzzled, 'Meat and two veg?'

'Yeah,' she continued, 'meat and two veg; one piece of meat, that's the centre of the meal – the centre of the universe – and a couple of vegetables thrown in for good luck. Oh yes, and a bit of gravy to help it go down.'

'Does everyone around here eat meat and two veg?' Alem asked, doubting the truth of what Pamela was saying.

'Yes – well, not everybody but most people. We are only about thirty miles from London but you'll find that London is a very different place,' Pamela said as her voice began to settle.

'I know, I went to London and it was very different. So much people, so many cars, so many big buildings and I only saw the parts where all the shops were.'

For the next ten minutes they let Alem talk to them about his impressions of London and how he had spent his evening in the West End with his father. Soon Mariam thought it was time for them to start talking to him.

'As I said before, Alem, we're from the Refugee Council. We know a little bit about how you came to be here and it's our job to make sure that you're looked after. We are not the police, we are not from the government and we don't have any special powers, but we are on your side.'

'We work with many people in the same situation,' Pamela interjected, 'so you have nothing to worry about.'

Mariam took out her notebook and began to make notes. 'We have to apply to what we call the Home Office for political-asylum. We need to get you this political asylum status so that you can stay in the country. Because we want to make sure that your wellbeing is protected and you get the best of what we have to offer, we have to ask you a few questions to start with. Now, if you're having problems with English you can speak in Amharic if you like.'

'I will try to speak in English,' Alem replied.

'OK,' Mariam said while making notes in her book. 'Can you tell us what happened before you came here? What made your father bring you here, and what was life like where you came from?'

'Yes, I will try my best.'

CHAPTER 3

~ This is War ~

My name is Alem Kelo. My age is fourteen. I am from Africa. I was born in an area called Badme. Some people think this area is a part of Eritrea and some people think that this area is a part of Ethiopia. My father taught me that it was a part of Africa and he said that there is no country in Africa that is bigger than Africa. In 1991 when the big war was over, I was five years old. My father and my mother and I went to live in Asmara. Asmara is a large city, the capital of Eritrea. My mother said we moved there so I could go to a good school and they could get better jobs. I did go to a good school there, it was a big school, a strong building. My mother and father did get good jobs; my mother worked in a court – she was the clerk – and my father worked in a post office. My father can speak six languages – Arabic, Afar, Tigrinya, Italian, English and Amharic. My mother can also speak these languages but I can only speak Amharic, Tigrinya and English. But I want to learn many more languages, and I want to make my English better. I did like Asmara, I had many friends there, but when I was ten years old we all went to live in Harar. Harar is in Ethiopia, high in the hills, the sun shines bright there but it is very cool. I found a new school and I had a good friend there, his name is Dawit. My mother found a new job in the bank and my father was the manager of the biggest post office in the city. He was the most important person there, and if there were problems everyone would have to come to him. We were happy living there until war broke out again and we began to have problems. Some of the other children at school started to pick on me, not Dawit but some others, and then one day my mother came home and said that she had lost her job because nobody did want to work with her. She said that the manager said she was causing too much trouble, the Ethiopian workers said that they are at war with Eritrea, so they will not work with someone from Eritrea. She was very upset. And then some weeks later my father said the people at work said that he must leave my mother because she is Eritrean and she is the enemy. My father said no, and he kept on working there but I think it was very difficult for him. Sometimes he came home from work and he didn't talk to us and I think this is because he was having problems at work. And then one night when we were asleep, the police broke down the door of our house and then they began to break up the house. They broke all the tables and chairs, and they told us to get ready to leave in the morning because buses would be taking us back to Eritrea. My father told them that he was born in Ethiopia, so they said that if he loves Ethiopia he can stay but me and my mother must go. My father said that he loves Ethiopia, he loves Eritrea and he loves Africa. One policeman then asked my father who would he fight for, and my father said he would fight for peace, and then the policeman hit my father with his rifle and my mother started to cry. When the police left we stayed awake all night and in the morning we went into the streets and we could see lots of people in the streets, many of them crying and getting on to buses. My father went to talk to a man and the man said he does not talk to traitors and then the police said that we must get on the bus right away and go to Eritrea, and my father said no. Then one policeman pushed my mother on the floor and my father got angry and shouted at him and the policeman pointed the rifle in my father's face and told him that we have fifteen minutes to go. So we went in our house and got as many things as we could, then we got on the bus and we went to Eritrea. The bus was full of Eritreans. When we went to Eritrea we stayed with my auntie. She is the sister of my mother. We had been there for about three months, then one day somebody was throwing some stones at my father when he was walking down the street. Then another day some women told my mother that she must leave my father and find a husband from Eritrea. In school in Eritrea the children started picking on me again and calling me Ethiopian, and one day after school some very big boys all started to beat me up when I was playing sport. They were very big, almost twenty years old. They beat my face and my stomach and when I was on the ground they just kept kicking me very hard. One boy said he was going to kick all the Ethiopian blood out of me. After this my mother and father were always talking about what they could do. They said Eritrea and Ethiopia were at war and our family is both Eritrean and Ethiopian. My mother said that we tried to live in both places and we always have problems. Then one day – it was my birthday – my father said I should have a holiday. He said that a holiday would make me happy and I will forget the problems. My mother was trying to find a job, she said she would not come, so my father took me to Djibouti by bus and from there we flew to Addis Ababa and from there we flew to England. I was thinking that we came here for a holiday, so that I could practise my English and see the buildings, but my father left me here so that I will not die.

CHAPTER 4

~ Asylum Seeking ~

When Alem stopped speaking the room fell silent. Mariam had witnessed the Ethiopia–Eritrea war herself and both she and Pamela had heard many horror stories of people fleeing war and persecution in the past, but they still found that no two stories were the same and each new story they heard still touched them.

Alem looked at them both and waited for a response, but there was none. 'Have I said something wrong?'

'No,' Pamela said quickly, 'no, not at all. You must say exactly what happened to you and your family. We need to know as much as possible about your experiences. Do you have any brothers or sisters?'

'No,' said Alem, shaking his head.

'Do you have any friends or family in England?' Mariam asked.

Alem continued shaking his head. 'No.'

Mariam looked towards the photo. 'Is that your mother and father?'

'Yes.'

'Your mother looks like a wise woman,' Mariam said, stretching forward to get a better view without leaving the chair, 'and she's beautiful.'

The photo was a posed one. Alem was seated on a chair with his mother and father standing behind him. His mother was dressed in a bright orange, flowered dress that would have looked very out of place in inner-city Britain. Her shoulders were draped with a light-green scarf. Her face was dark and slim with a slightly pointed chin and gently smiling lips. Large earrings hung from her ears and her hair was plaited close to her head in rows going from the front to the back.

'You look like a great family, there is a lot of love in that photo,' Mariam observed. 'Do you have a phone back home?'

'No,' Alem said, looking at the photo.

'That's fine. Enough for now,' said Mariam.

'One last question,' Pamela said as she stood up. 'Do you want something to eat?'

'Yes,' Alem said hesitantly.

'What kind of food would you like?' she continued.

'Italian, Italian,' Alem said with a hint of a smile on his face.

Pamela was a little surprised. 'Italian?' she said, looking towards Mariam.

'If the man said he wants Italian, then the man gets Italian,' Mariam insisted. She looked around the room. There wasn't much in the way of personal belongings. 'How much luggage do you have?'

'Only one bag,' Alem replied, 'one small bag.'

'Well,' Mariam said, 'you have to leave this hotel today, so what we'd like you to do is pack your bag now and come with us. The first thing we'll do is to go and find some Italian food and then we'll take you back to our office. At the office we'll work out a plan and get you somewhere to stay.'

Alem went to the wardrobe, got his bag and put his few items of clothing in it. Then he went around the room and collected the photo and his schoolbooks and put them away too. He went to the bathroom and collected his toiletry bag and put that in his bag before zipping it up. The whole packing process took less than five minutes.

They left the hotel after saying their goodbyes to Mr Hardwick and then rode for forty minutes in Mariam's slow old Volkswagen to Reading town centre. There they found an Italian restaurant where Alem indulged himself with a very large portion of spaghetti bolognese while Mariam and Pamela slowly grazed on some boiled vegetables and pasta. It was in their plan not to bother Alem with questions over the meal; instead they let him eat, only interrupting him periodically to ask him how the food was or if he wanted more.

After the meal they took a five-minute drive to their offices, which consisted of four rooms above a shoe shop. Every corner had a desk with a computer on it, as well as stacks of paper. Most of the desks were in use. Mariam introduced Alem to every worker, clearly stating their name and whether they were full-time, part-time or voluntary workers. Then he was taken into a small room, which was empty except for a round table with four chairs. As Alem entered the room he wondered why he was introduced to everyone. Was it for a purpose? He worried because less than one minute after the introductions ended he couldn't remember one single name. The names all sounded strange and unmemorable to him.

As they sat down, one of the workers came in carrying a tray with a pot of tea, cups, milk, sugar and biscuits on it. The worker put it on the table and left the room.

'Would you like a cup of tea?' Pamela asked as she began to prepare the cups.

'No, thank you,' Alem replied.

'Would you like some biscuits then?'

'No, thank you, I have no more room inside me. I'm full up.'

When the tea making was done, Mariam began the talking as Pamela made notes.

'Right, Alem, as we said earlier, this organisation is called the Refugee Council. We are independent and our main concern is to look after the interests of refugees. Unfortunately it's not up to us whether you can stay in Britain but we will try our best to make sure that the Home Office knows why you should stay.'

Once again Alem looked puzzled. 'I don't want to stay,' he said. 'I don't really want to stay here, I want to go home – to Africa.'

Mariam responded quickly. 'But you know why your father and mother had to get you out, don't you?'

'Of course I do, I told you why, but I don't want to stay here for ever. It's cold.'

Mariam smiled. 'Yes, we know it's cold and we hope that you don't have to stay here for ever, but do you really want to go home right now? Do you think it's safe?'

There was a long silence before Alem replied. He took time to think through his answer and as he answered he placed every word carefully. 'I want to go home but I can't go now because of the fighting. So I would like to go home when there is peace. Most of all I want to be with my parents.'

'We understand completely,' Mariam replied. 'Let me explain something to you, Alem. It's important that you understand this. We have to make an application for you to stay; we have to get permission. That permission has to come from the Home Office.

The Home Office is a part of the government. These things can take some time but it has to be done, otherwise you will get into trouble with the police. Today we'll fill in a form for you. That form will go to the Home Office and then they will decide what to do; they may want you to attend a hearing or they may ask you to see them for an interview. If they do, you'll see that their interviewers are very different from ours. They will ask you a lot of difficult questions, and they sometimes ask the same questions over and over again to catch you out, and they certainly won't take you out for a meal; but it won't be too bad if you are prepared.'

Alem sat up in his seat and said very confidently, 'OK, I am prepared.'

Pamela handed a form to Mariam, who began filling it in, stopping sometimes to ask Alem questions but mainly working from knowledge that she already had. The main purpose of the form was to confirm the fact that the applicant wanted to apply for asylum so it did not go into detail over the circumstances. What it did do was to ask the applicant's name, age, country of origin and whether the applicant was under the age of sixteen, and if so, was he or she accompanied by an adult? Alem could see by how fast Mariam ticked some of the boxes that she had done this many times before. She finished by repeating some of the questions and answers to Alem to check that she had replied correctly, then she asked him to sign the form. Alem could sense how important the form was when Mariam looked it over one more time before signing it herself. Without taking her eyes off the form, she handed it to Pamela and watched as she signed it.

After signing it, Pamela put it with the rest of the documents into her folder and began to leave the room. 'I'll get this on its way.'

Mariam also stood up to leave. 'Wait here, Alem, I'll be back in a moment. I have to find somewhere for you to stay.'

By now Alem was sure that the two women were on his side, but as he sat waiting in the empty room, he couldn't help thinking that they must be talking about him. He knew now that he had nothing to fear from them but still he was curious to know what conversations were going on behind the scenes. He could hear talk in the background but couldn't make out what they were saying. Frustrated, he got up and put his ear to the door to see if he could hear more. He also had to listen for anyone approaching the door, so he still could not hear much but he did hear Mariam say his name in what sounded like a telephone conversation.

He sat down and waited for another ten minutes before Mariam re-entered the room alone. 'Right,

Alem,' she said as she sat down. 'I've found a place for you to stay for a while. It's an OK place, clean, not very far from here, and there are not too many boys there.'

'What do you mean, not too many boys there?' Alem replied.

'I mean that it's not too overcrowded. Some of these places have hundreds of boys in them, but this one's not so bad.'

Alem was really confused. 'Is this a hotel just for boys?'

'No, not really, Alem, this is not a hotel, this is more like a hostel, actually it's a children's home. Because of your age you will have to go into the care of the local authority – the municipality. They will look after you, but we'll be visiting you all the time. We'll visit you as much as we can and we'll get a social worker, someone whose job is to make sure you have no problems.'

Alem leaned over the table and said, 'Kanchi gar menor ichilallehu wey?'

'No, I'm sorry, Alem. I would love you to stay with me but it's not possible. For the time being you must go into care or we could all get into trouble. We're going to try our best to make sure that you don't stay there too long and we're going to make sure you're looked after, but you have to go.'

'What kind of boys are there?'

'All different kinds of boys – big, small, black and white.'

'Where do they come from?'

'Well, I haven't been there for a long time but you usually find that they come from everywhere, different parts of Britain but also from other countries.'

'What is the food like?'

Mariam paused for a moment. 'I don't really know. It's probably the meat-and-two-veg type but don't worry, we'll try and get some of the food that you like sometimes. I'm sure we can organise some spaghetti,' she said smiling.

Alem exhaled hard as if he had been holding his breath. He spoke as if defeated. 'OK, I will go there for now, but please, will you help me if somebody hurts me or if something goes wrong?'

'Of course,' Mariam replied, 'but listen, these people want to look after you. It may not be the best place in the world. If they had better buildings and more money, things would be better, but you are in care and they want to care for you. We will of course help you if you need help.'

Alem thought for a while. 'I know; maybe I could design a better building for them so that when they get the money the new plans are finished.'

'Yes, of course,' Mariam said as she stood up, 'and when you've finished designing their new building, do you think you could design new offices for us?'

CHAPTER 5

~ Welcome Home ~

The children's home was situated on the outskirts of Reading. It was an old building that had been through many uses. It had originally been built and owned by a wealthy merchant, who had sold it when he could no longer afford to run four mansions. Since then it had been used as a tuberculosis isolation hospital, a home for the elderly, a yoga retreat and a borstal. The moment Alem arrived, he hated it, although it was the kind of building that he could have really liked. It had a long drive leading to it, and with the knowledge Alem had gained from reading books on architecture he guessed it was Victorian. Two large stone lions guarded the main doors and much of the grey stonework was covered with creeping ivy. The green surroundings were idyllic but Alem just had a bad feeling about the place. It was as if he knew that the place had a pretty bleak history. Something made him feel that he wasn't going to be having a great time there.

Mariam stayed for only fifteen minutes before saying goodbye and promising to visit Alem soon. It was left to Sarah Cohen, a middle-aged blonde woman, to introduce him to his new home.

'We have eighty-six boys staying here and I know the name of every one of them,' she said proudly. 'My name is Sarah and there are another seven members of staff here. All the boys call us by our first names. The staff are never all here at the same time, of course, some prefer night duty, some the day shift, but you should find that all the staff are friendly and willing to help you.'

Alem showed no emotion as he looked around the drab office. He had only one thing on his mind and he said it: 'When am I leaving here?'

'I must be completely honest with you now: I don't know – no one knows. What I do know is that Mariam and her colleagues will try their best to make sure that you don't stay here a moment longer than you need to – but while you are here I promise that we will try to make you as comfortable as possible.'

Alem heard the sounds that came from her mouth but he was not listening to her and she knew it.

'Come on,' she said, 'bring your bag, I'll show you around.'

They left the office and began to walk the timber-panelled corridors. In places the highly polished wooden floor creaked and as they progressed Alem began to hear activity in the distance.

'The staff offices are out of bounds to the boys –

unless they are invited, of course – but most of the staff spend very little time in the offices anyway.'

They turned a corner and she opened a side door. The noise hit Alem; it was like an explosive attack upon his ears. The large room was full of boys. In one corner four boys played table football with a small group cheering them on. In another corner a group of boys took turns using hand-held consoles to play each other at Streetfighter on a television screen. Two boys were chasing each other around the room for no apparent reason, while others watched a football match on another television. On the other side of the room, board games were being played and other boys just stood around shouting at each other. From all this tumult two male adults emerged and headed towards Alem and Sarah. Sarah had fully entered the room but Alem still stood near the door.

'Come in, Alem,' said one of the men as he stretched his hand out towards him.

Alem was surprised by the man's very casual use of his name. Alem lifted his right hand nervously, he wasn't used to shaking the hands of adults, but he went for it. The man shook vigorously, too vigorously for Alem's liking.

'My name's Tom, Tom Whittaker but the boys just call me Tom. How are you?'

'I am fine, thank you,' Alem replied unhappily.

Tom was in his late forties, his brown hair tinged

with grey. He was wearing purple corduroys that looked as if they had been handed down from one generation to another and a large black and white jumper that looked as if he had wrapped a whole sheep around himself. He looked genuinely excited to see Alem, which made Alem worried; he wasn't in the mood for excitement.

'Well, Alem,' Tom said, looking around the room, 'these guys may look wild but they're all right when you get to know them; we have our problems but who doesn't?'

The other man stretched out his hand. He was in his late twenties, in jeans and a sweatshirt, and had completely shaved off his hair.

'Hello, my name's Dave.'

Alem shook his hand.

'I'm new here, so we're kind of in the same boat. It's only my second day.'

Alem had another glance around. Since leaving Eritrea he had not seen so many young people in one place. He realised how much he missed the sound of his own generation but he wondered how he would get on with these teenagers, they all seemed so confident. He could see that the boys came from all racial backgrounds, he had never seen such a mix of boys in one place. Then he saw one boy who was alone, sitting on a chair away from the other boys just staring at the wall in front of him with his eyes wide open.

Tom noticed that Alem was looking at the boy. 'That's Mustafa, nice boy but he's a bit of a loner,' Tom said.

Sarah began her tour-guide routine. 'This is the recreation room, most of us spend most of our time here. Some of the boys have gone on a hill climb for a couple of days but they'll be back tomorrow. Anyway, this is where the action happens. We have a variety of things to keep you occupied and we always welcome ideas to keep the boys busy.'

'See you later,' said Tom.

'Take it easy,' said Dave and they both walked off, leaving Sarah to it.

'We're very open-minded here,' Sarah continued, 'but we only allow smoking in the smoke room for those that are over sixteen. We don't allow knives on the premises and mobile phones will be confiscated, alcohol is not allowed and we will not tolerate drugs of any kind – in fact if anyone is caught breaking the law, the law says that we should report them to the police, and we do.'

She turned and walked past Alem back into the corridor. 'Come along, I'll show you where you'll be sleeping.'

She pointed out the toilets and a small room known as the quiet room where boys could sit and read. There were no books or boys in there. Then she opened another door. 'This is the smoking room.'

Three older-looking boys looked towards them from the smoke-filled room.

'Hello, boys, this is Alem,' she said, waving the smoke away from her face.

One boy raised his hand. Alem wasn't sure whether he was saying hello or waving them away. Another just pulled on his cigarette, and the third one smiled wickedly and said, 'All right?'

'Yes,' Alem replied, trying not to breathe in too deeply.

'We'll soon see to that,' the boy replied, nodding his head in assent to a question that had not been asked.

'Very funny,' Sarah replied, closing the door and continuing the tour.

Upstairs, Alem was taken into a large room with about fifteen beds in it. Alem looked horrified, he hated the idea of sleeping in a room with so many others.

'This is the large dormitory,' said Sarah. 'Some boys like being together like this and that's OK as long as they behave. This is the biggest room we have but it doesn't suit everyone, of course. Follow me.'

She walked into another room, which was much smaller, with only two beds. 'This is where you will be staying. You'll be sharing with one other boy, a nice boy about your age.'

She walked over to a bedside locker and patted it as

if it were a docile pet. 'This is your personal locker. You will have your own key but if you have anything really valuable you should let us keep it in the office.'

Alem had absolutely nothing to say. He hadn't known what to expect but he didn't expect this. He kicked his bag under his bed.

'OK?' said Sarah. There was no reply. She tried again louder. 'Is that OK, Alem? Do you have any questions?'

Alem just shook his head and looked downwards.

'Good,' she said cheerfully. 'It's almost time for our late snack, then you'll have a chance to meet some of the other boys. Soon after the snack it's bedtime, it's a pretty straightforward routine. By tomorrow dinner-time I'm sure you'll have made a few friends. It's always difficult to get used to a place like this, it takes time.'

The late snack wasn't anything special and Alem didn't want anything anyway. Tom and Dave took digestive biscuits and tea around on trays to the boys in the recreation room but when Tom offered Alem some, he declined. Alem watched as the boys ate their biscuits and drank their tea. As he watched, he was approached by one of the boys he had seen earlier in the smoke room, the one who made the remark to him.

'Get some biscuits,' he said, nodding his head in

the direction of Tom.

'I don't want any,' Alem replied.

'Get some biscuits,' the boy insisted, 'and bring them to me. Now.'

Alem was still unmoved. He just replied very calmly, 'I don't want any biscuits. If you want biscuits you get them for yourself.'

Two other boys now joined in; Alem recognised them, they were both in the smoke room earlier. 'Get the biscuits, it's the easy way out,' one of them said as he looked Alem up and down.

'You'll get me some biscuits or I'll bust you up,' said the first kid loudly, loud enough for Tom to hear.

Tom walked over. 'Right, so what's the problem here?' he asked.

'Nothing,' said the first boy while the two others quickly walked away. 'I was just welcoming the new boy, you know how it is, Tom, new kid on the block, needs a bit of guidance.'

'Of course, why didn't I think of that?' he asked sarcastically. 'So why are you shouting? And didn't I hear you say something about biscuits?'

'I don't think so,' said the boy smiling.

'I think so,' said Tom smiling back. 'Alem – you tell me what happened.'

Alem was as straightforward as he could get. 'I was standing here on my own, he came up to me and asked me to get some biscuits. I told him that I didn't want any and he said that I should get some biscuits for him. I kept telling him that I will not get any biscuits. Then his friend told me to get some and he shouted at me,' said Alem while pointing to the boy in front of him. 'And then you heard him and you came.'

The boy looked straight at Alem, amazed that he had the guts to tell all. Alem just looked back at him unmoved.

'Apologise,' said Tom to the boy, 'apologise now.'

The boy was still staring at Alem when he replied unconvincingly, 'I'm sorry.'

'Right,' said Tom, 'and I don't want to hear of you trying to get someone's biscuits again. If someone wants to get their share and give it away, that's fine. But you can't force them to give you anything, even if they don't want it themselves. Have you got that?'

'Yeah,' the boy replied quietly.

'OK, you can go now,' said Tom pointing him away.

The boy walked away with a swagger.

'Are you OK?' Tom asked.

'Yes,' said Alem, and walked away to a relatively quiet part of the room.

About fifteen minutes later the three boys appeared right in front of Alem as he watched some boys playing the computer game.

'You're dead,' said the main boy, the boy who had kept telling Alem to get the biscuits. 'You are dead meat, that's all I'm saying now, you've had it.'

When they were a safe distance away, Alem watched them carefully, checking out their size. They were much bigger than him but he knew that he should not be intimidated by them. He clenched his fists defiantly and continued to watch the computer game.

At ten o'clock they were all instructed to stop what they were doing and go to bed. Alem had still made no friends, only enemies. When he arrived at his room, he found a boy there. The boy was sitting on his bed playing with a Gameboy. He stopped when he saw Alem.

'What's your name?' the boy asked.

'My name is Alem Kelo,' he replied. 'What's yours?'

'My name is Stanley Burton.' Then he began to speak frantically without a pause. 'I've been here for ten months, they told me I wouldn't stay here long but I've been here for ten months. I hate it here, they're mean. Some boys just disappear from here and nobody knows where they go. They just disappear, like; you know what I mean? My father died in the war, the Gulf War, the newspaper said he died like a hero, I want to die like a hero, I want to die like my dad, I don't want to die yet but when I do die I want to die like a hero. Get my picture in the paper and

I mean? My mother ain't dead, she's alive but the doctor said she can't cope. That's why she didn't feed me or send me to school, she couldn't cope. She's in a place like this too, only that one's for big people, and my sister, she's in a place like this too, only that one's a place for girls.'

Alem thought that he had to do something to bring this verbal marathon to a halt. He grabbed his bag, removed his toothbrush and said, 'Excuse me, I must go to the bathroom,' as he shot out of the room to the toilet and shower area.

It was the quickest Alem had moved all day. He looked for a sink to wash his face and clean his teeth but they were all busy, with boys waiting. They were noisy, telling jokes that Alem couldn't understand. No one made an attempt to speak to him, yet he thought that he was the one that everyone was joking about.

Then Mustafa, the loner that Alem had noticed in the recreation room before, came up to him. He looked African, Alem thought, but not Ethiopian. The boy looked quite seriously at Alem. 'Watch out, man, Sweeney is going to get you. Just watch yu back and don't mek him tek any liberties wid yu.'

Mustafa walked away. Alem looked around and decided that he wasn't going to wait around any longer, so he began to make his way to his room without washing.

Back in the room Stanley was already in bed. He

lay on his back looking silently up at the ceiling. Alem tried to go about the business of getting into bed without disturbing him. He removed the family photo from his bag, got undressed and put on the worn-out but clean pyjamas that had been left out on the bed for him. Just as he got into bed, Stanley verbally took off again.

'The lights will go off in ten minutes unless you want to turn them off yourself but I usually wait for a member of staff. The staff don't do much here, they just walk around, like, so let them work, that's what I say. Have you ever been in a helicopter? I have on the army base; we used to live on the army base, you know. Have you ever touched a gun? I have –'

'OK, that's enough,' came a voice from the doorway. It was Dave. 'Are you all right Alem?'

'Yes,' Alem replied.

'Don't let him talk you to death. If you let him, he'll talk to you all night. All you have to do is to tell him to stop and he'll stop. He never gets offended. I'll put your lights off now if that's all right with you guys.'

The boys didn't reply and the lights went off. 'Good night,' said Dave, 'see you tomorrow evening.'

Alem listened in the dark, holding the photo to his chest, as the doors were closed up and down the corridors and Dave and Tom bid everyone good night. When they had gone, whispers and giggles could still be heard coming from some of the rooms, especially the large dormitory, but soon it all died down to silence and Alem fell asleep.

The day had been a long one so Alem had no problem sleeping, until deep in the night when he was woken up by the sound of Stanley crying and talking in his sleep.

'No, please don't! I haven't done anything, Mummy. Please don't lock me in my room, I don't like it in my room, Mummy, don't, please don't!'

Alem tried to stay still but Stanley got louder.

'Don't go, Mummy, please don't go, Mummy. When are you coming back? Don't leave me in here all on my own! I love you Mummy. Please don't – Mummy I'm going to jump out of the window, Mummy, come back, it's dark, Mummy look – I'm going to die.' Then he screamed, 'Somebody help me!' as he jolted upwards. He sat up and opened his eyes.

Alem couldn't see him in the dark but he could hear him trying to get his breath back. Alem listened as Stanley composed himself, lay down and took a deep breath before trying to go back to sleep.

Silence fell upon the room once more, but just before Stanley fell asleep he took one last deep breath and said, 'Mummy, it's so dark, Mummy, please come back soon.'

CHAPTER 6

~ Meet the Lads ~

The call of 'Good morning, boys' echoing from the corridor woke Alem up at seven. The first thing he did was to make sure he still had his photo and check to see whether Stanley was all right. Stanley was very quiet. He put a thumb up to Alem, smiled and got out of bed as if nothing had happened.

Another female member of staff knocked on the door and entered the room. 'Good morning, boys,' she said. 'How are you today, Stanley?'

'I'm happy, Maureen,' Stanley replied.

'Did you sleep well, Stanley?'

'I don't know,' he said.

She turned to Alem. 'And you must be the new boy – Alem. Good morning, Alem,' she said, almost skipping away to the next room.

Alem put the photo in his bag and followed the crowd. This time he managed to get a wash and then they went down for breakfast in the large dining hall. First the boys had to line up and choose their meal. They could have bacon, eggs, toast, sausages, tomatoes and cornflakes in any combination. The tables were laid out in three parallel lines. The boys were watched over by three members of staff, the bubbly posh lady who had woken Alem up and two men whom Alem had not seen before. Alem was just not sure what to eat; it was food but not food as he knew it. He played it safe and had toast and tea. He wasn't sure where to sit and for a while he stood with his tray looking for a place until he spotted Mustafa, the boy who had given him the warning about Sweeney. The seat next to Mustafa was empty so Alem went and sat next to him.

'Is it OK if I sit here, please?'

'No worries, yu safe,' Mustafa replied.

A boy on the other side of the seat just glanced at Alem before tucking back into his breakfast.

Mustafa began speaking to Alem as if he was simply continuing the conversation from the night before. 'I ain't trying to frighten ya, yu know. I am just telling yu, guy, yu have to watch out.'

Alem nodded his head in reply.

Mustafa continued, 'Thing with dat Sweeney is dat if you let him get away with stuff, he'll keep coming back to you.' He pointed his finger to someone at the other table. 'You see him?'

'Yes,' Alem replied, 'I share a room with him.'

'He's Stanley. Sweeney beat him up once and now every time Sweeney wants extra biscuits or toast or anything, Stanley gives it to him. Shame, man. Sweeney troubled me once and me and him fight, yu check? I would of buss him up if staff never come but he don't mess with me now. Stanley's soft.'

'He talks so much,' Alem replied.

'For sure, if yu let him talk he'll just talk yu crazy. I actually see him talk a guy to sleep. For real. He's weird but it's not his fault. His dad died in the Gulf War.'

'The Gulf?' Alem said, looking down into his breakfast while trying to make sense of it. 'Why the Gulf, why Aden?'

'No,' Mustafa slowed down. 'Not the Gulf of Aden. Dat boy's father died in the Persian Gulf War – yu know, Saddam Hussein – Iraq – Kuwait. It's in the Middle East and Britain fought there with the Americans and them, and that's where his father died.'

'Oh, that's sad,' Alem said, feeling for Stanley but trying hard not to think of the war he himself had left behind.

'That's not all, man,' Mustafa continued. 'When his father died, his mother lost it, she went loco, loony. She used to lock him up for hours in his room and sometimes if he cried too much she would take the light bulbs out and leave him in the dark. Could you imagine that, man? Left in the dark for hours, serious hours, yu know, sometimes she would be gone all night, and sometimes he was starving to death. Wickedness, man, pure wickedness.'

Alem looked towards Stanley, who was talking

66

away to someone. He felt that he understood him a little bit more now and he was trying to think of something he could say to him, some words of comfort. Then he thought he might get plenty of time for that later and anyway he couldn't really go up to him and say that he knew his life story.

Mustafa spoke again. 'He's weird, he don't harm no one but he's weird.'

'He had a very bad dream last night,' Alem said, chewing on his toast.

'Bad dream?' Mustafa replied. 'Dat guy has nightmares, dat guy wakes up screaming his head off in the night. He even goes sleepwalking. He walks in his sleep talking to his mother. I don't wanna frighten yu, but everyone knows it.'

'What's your name again?' Alem asked in an abrupt change of subject. 'I was told but I forgot.'

'Mustafa,' the boy replied proudly, 'and you're Alem, I know.'

The boys then got down to their breakfasts. Alem was feeling very much wiser for the conversation and wondering whether he had found a friend in Mustafa.

After breakfast all the boys returned upstairs to brush their teeth and make their beds. Alem spoke very little to Stanley, not wanting to start him off on another rant, although he did ask him what would be happening next. Stanley told him that all they had to do now was to go to the recreation room. If there were any special jobs to be done, boys would be picked from there, or maybe there would be a trip somewhere, but boys who went on trips would have had to be there for a little longer than one day.

Alem finished making his bed and went down to the recreation room. Once again he found himself just standing around alone watching the other boys. They seemed to be playing the same games in the same groups. It felt to Alem as if he hadn't been to sleep at all, nothing had changed except for the staff members. The only time that any of the boys spoke to Alem was when the table football flew off the table and Alem handed it back to one of them. All they said was 'Cheers' but it was enough to keep Alem's mind busy wondering what 'cheers' meant. Then there was Mustafa, but he tended to sit alone most of the time looking out of the window

As Alem went to walk away to venture elsewhere in the room, someone bumped into him from the side.

'Sorry, mate, but I meant it.'

It was Sweeney and his two friends. Alem tried several times to walk away but one of them would block him each time he tried. He wanted to avoid panicking, conscious that he was in a room full of people. He looked around for help. Everyone was doing their thing, and those that did catch a glimpse of the stand-off just looked away as if seeing nothing. Mustafa was unaware of what was happening.

'Right,' said Sweeney, placing himself right in front of Alem. 'Yu mess with me already, right, now I'm gonna show yu dat yu can't mess with me again. But first I'm gonna give yu a chance. Today we have wonderful cod and chips and beautiful broccoli for dinner. All I want you to do is give me your cod and chips, and you can enjoy yu broccoli in peace. It won't make me and you best friends, but life will be much easier for you.'

Alem tried to show no fear. 'You will have your own chips and if there's some left over you can get some more. Why do you want my chips?'

Sweeney took a step forward, placing himself inches away from Alem. As he spoke into Alem's face, Alem could smell his bacon breath. Even at this time of danger, Alem's mind still found a moment to think, 'This boy has not cleaned his teeth.'

'I want your chips, that's all you need to know,' Sweeney said, smiling wickedly and breathing all over Alem's face.

'Well, I don't think I'm having any dinner,' Alem replied in an attempt to outsmart him.

'Well,' Sweeney said, spraying bacon-flavoured saliva over Alem's face, 'that's even better, you have nothing to lose then, do you? Just get the cod and chips and give them to me, and that will save you from getting a kicking, won't it?'

Sweeney spoke fast. Alem didn't catch all that he

said but he had his principles and he was going to stick to them. 'I don't care what you say, I am not giving you any food.'

The moment Alem finished his sentence, Sweeney struck him with his fist in the solar plexus. Alem's breath was completely taken away and as he went down Sweeney kicked him under his chin, causing him to bite his tongue. The pain was excruciating. Alem just wasn't prepared. All he could do at that moment was cling on to Sweeney's legs. Sweeney was unable to kick but he rained down a whole heap of punches over Alem's head and back. Alem could hear other boys cheering Sweeney on; he couldn't understand why no one was coming to his rescue. He clung on for dear life but the shouting got louder and the punches increased. Quickly, Alem had a change of heart. He had to defend himself; he could no longer be passive. He held on to Sweeney's feet with one hand, then used his other hand to push him over. Sweeney fell. There was now a scrap on the floor. They traded kicks and punches at a rate of six per second. Alem noticed that he was feeling extra kicks, kicks that weren't coming from Sweeney, but there was nothing that he could do about them, he just tried his best to deal with the aggressor in hand. Suddenly Alem felt a change in the action, it was Mustafa, and he wasn't fighting but trying to separate them.

Just then came those immortal words, 'Break it up,

lads, that's enough.' Mustafa backed off and the two male members of staff began pulling them apart, but the two boys still desperately tried to kick and punch each other as if the last punch was a matter of pride.

They were eventually separated and both panted hard for breath, even though, like most fights, it had actually lasted about one minute. As they were being held back from each other, Alem stayed silent, still not confident enough to speak English and fight at the same time. Sweeney shouted threats as if he had rehearsed them hundreds of times before:

'I'll kill you, yu bastard – yu don't mess with me and get away with it – I'll turn yu lights out – you are dead – yu understand – yu dead meat – I mean really dead.'

Alem was quite shocked by the whole episode. It happened so suddenly, so unexpectedly, but what for? Alem's biggest pain still came from the first punch to his stomach. He looked at Sweeney, whose nose was bleeding, and said, 'You do all this for some chips?'

They were both taken to the staff room and given the usual warnings, except they couldn't be threatened with detention or extra homework. Sweeney was warned that he had a report being prepared for a court case and that he needed to be on his best behaviour. Alem was told not to use violence to overcome violence, but to report all violent acts to a member of staff. This was rubbish, of course, and Alem knew it. He was tempted to ask how practical it was to report an act of violence just after you've been winded, considering how quickly the next kick follows up, but he decided not to.

For the rest of the day Alem felt miserable. He spoke very little to anyone and no one made an effort to speak to him. Only Mustafa asked if he was OK and said he was sorry about what happened and that he did warn him about Sweeney. Stanley wanted to talk for hours about the type of gun he planned to buy, but Alem decided to walk away and leave him talking to himself. One or two of the other boys saw him and said no more than 'All right?' But Alem knew by now that when most people said 'All right?' they didn't really mean, 'are you all right?' He thought this was a gross misuse of the language, he just couldn't understand how they could say 'All right?' and walk away without waiting for an answer.

What made the rest of the day difficult was Sweeney and his two friends. Every time they saw him they gave him dirty looks, and every time they were near him they threatened him. At the dinner table Alem had nothing to eat, but Sweeney came over to him all the same to tell him that they still had unfinished business. Alem didn't say a word. He hardly said a word for the rest of that day. By now he had decided that words weren't enough, now was the time for action.

CHAPTER 7

~ The Road to Nowhere ~

Early that evening, a minibus arrived at the home. It was a group of boys returning from their hill-climbing adventure. Tom and Dave were back on duty. Dave stayed in the recreation room while Tom went to help the boys unload.

Alem saw an opportunity. He walked as quickly as he could up to his room and packed his little bag, then he secretly made his way back downstairs, knowing that he couldn't afford to be seen carrying the bag. He stopped to look around every corner before turning it, listening for the slightest sign of anyone approaching. Eventually he found his way to the very back of the building where a door led to the large garden area. It was dark. He tried to open the door using the handle but it was locked, he then tried various bolts and catches on the door but to no avail. Then in desperation he resorted to shaking it but the door remained locked.

Alem lacked a real plan and was making it up as he went along, and he certainly didn't have a back-up plan. He searched his mind quickly for ideas but he didn't know the building well enough. He noticed a door barely visible in the darkness. He turned the handle and it opened. As he walked in, he kicked something with his feet; it felt like a cardboard box. Bending down to check, he knocked something else, something hard and metallic which fell crashing to the floor, breaking the silence. He tried to turn and make his way out, as he did that he rested his hand on a shelf, the shelf collapsed and all that was on it came raining down.

Alem stood still and let the crescendo happen around him. He was now sure that he would be caught. He realised that he was in a broom cupboard, and he thought he was in trouble. But when the last bucket stopped rolling and silence returned, no one came running. No one had heard a thing. Probably, Alem thought, because the cupboard was so far away from the offices and the recreation room. Then there were all the games being played and the boys arriving from their trip. Alem noticed a small window in the broom cupboard; maybe he still had a chance.

He gripped his bag. Movement was difficult and noisy because of the things under his feet but he made it to the window. Standing on a vacuum cleaner to reach it, he could just see the garden at the back. He opened the window and threw the bag out, realising that this was the point of no return. He just about managed to squeeze through the window headfirst, and clinging to the window frame he manoeuvred himself around and managed to jump down and land on his feet. As he landed he froze, still listening for any sign of a raised alarm. When he thought it was safe he picked up his bag and began his escape.

The house stood in three acres of land. The garden near the house soon turned into wild, unkempt woods. Alem struggled through it. It was crispy cold; every footstep crunched on the ground as dried twigs broke. He could hear clearly every breath he took, and the cold wind was burning his face unlike any kind of cold that he had felt before. He looked behind and could see the light reflecting from the house; his only thought was that he should get as far away as possible from that house and its reflection.

After fifteen minutes he came to the boundary fence. It was about six feet high. He climbed halfway up, threw his bag over and then proceeded to climb the rest. When he reached the top he tried to grip the fence, only to find that it was barbed wire. He shouted out in pain, then he stopped, balanced precariously on the fence, hoping no one had heard his shout. He jumped down on the other side and fell on his back on the ground, where he lay for a moment in a tired celebration of leaving the grounds. He didn't know where he was, he didn't know where he was going, and he could feel the small but painful cuts on his hand. Although he had lost all sense of direction, at least he was on a well-trodden path that had to lead to some-where else. He took a couple of deep breaths, picked himself up, grabbed his bag and proceeded to walk.

Soon he came to a road. It had no pavement, no lights and no markings. He waited for a couple of minutes but he didn't even see a car. Looking left and right in the darkness made no difference, the darkness in both directions looked identical. For no reason at all he went left.

After walking for over an hour, his feet began to hurt and the bag that at first seemed so light had gradually become a very heavy burden. He carried it in alternating hands in order to ease the burden, but as the night continued, the bag just seemed to increase in weight. The road twisted and turned. Alem had lost all sense of time and place and was now quietly praying that a city, a town or village would be nearby. He was hungry and exhausted; how he wished that he had eaten more!

At this point he decided that he needed somewhere to rest. Sick of walking, sick of the cold and sick of the dark, he took a risk and left the road by forcing his way through a hedge. Now he was walking across fields. He knew that he was doing something wrong, possibly illegal, so he tried to ease his conscience by causing as little damage to the crops as possible.

Fifteen minutes after leaving the road he came upon a house with the lights still on. He stood looking at the house, wondering if he should knock, when he noticed at the edge of the field a barn-type building. That's it, he thought, I shall stay in there. He made his way to the building, keeping his head as low as he could. It was a large wooden barn with large doors that were unlocked. He opened one very slightly and entered but he could see nothing inside. He began to feel his way around. Everything was dirty and muddy, he could feel cold metal; the barn was full of vehicles and machinery. In the centre of the barn he came across a big wheel, one of the wheels of a large tractor. Next to the wheel he felt a step, he climbed up and found his way into the cabin. It wasn't warm but it was dry, and at least it wasn't as cold as outside. The driver's seat was reasonably comfortable and he thought that it was high enough off the ground to make it difficult for any hyenas or snakes to get him. He closed the cabin door, fiddled in his bag to find his extra shirt, put it on and then he fell asleep in the driving position.

In the morning he woke up to the sound of children laughing. He was quite high up, looking down at the various strange pieces of machinery in the barn. Realising that he couldn't hang around, he quickly grabbed his bag and climbed down. He peeped out of the door to see three children getting into a large Land Rover jeep, which had a woman in the driver's seat. Alem presumed this was a mother taking her children to school. Soon all the children were in the vehicle and they were driving away. He wanted to head down the same path that the Land Rover had gone down, as he thought that it might lead to a major road. But to get to the path he would have to pass the house. He left the barn and made his way to the path, keeping low and hiding behind farm vehicles, hedges and walls as he went.

As he sneaked past the house he saw nobody and he thought that no one saw him until he heard, 'Hey, you! What the hell are you doing here?'

It was the voice of a man from inside the house. Alem didn't hang around, he ran down the path as fast as he could. Then he could hear the man on the stone-flagged path outside the house.

'You're lucky you ain't been shot, lad. Watch out, the police will be after you!'

Alem just ran and ran without stopping or looking back until he came to a road. It was another quiet road that was very steep. He walked up it. Cars passed him periodically. All the drivers really stared at him. He knew he looked out of place and he could see no one else walking these roads.

On reaching the top of the hill he stopped to rest his legs. He looked around and was dismayed and angry by what he saw. There, right in front of him, was the drive to the children's home. He threw his bag down on the ground and burst into tears, crying quietly. He had done nothing but go around in a large circle. At no point was he more than half a mile away from the home. Now he was too tired to keep running. Silently acknowledging defeat and in desperate need of food, he began walking up the path.

Back in the home he was kept in the staff room, where Sarah Cohen washed and cleaned his cuts and gave him breakfast. Sarah had heard about the fight on the previous night, which Alem was unwilling to talk about; he just insisted on being moved from the home. Soon Mariam turned up with another young woman.

'Alem, you poor thing!' Mariam said. 'What's wrong?'

Alem sat in a high-backed chair with his bag at his side. 'I don't want to stay here,' he replied, looking out of the window down the drive.

The young woman left the room with the other two members of staff, leaving Mariam and Alem alone.

'So what's the matter, Alem? Everyone was really worried about you. Why did you run away?'

'I hate it here,' Alem said. 'Nobody talks to me, everyone is so strange, and people want to fight me. I was beaten up in schools in Africa, do you think I want to be beat up here as well? You know, these people are rubbish. Let me tell you something – they love to fight, yes, but these people are not fighting for land, they are not fighting for justice or their beliefs, these stupid boys are fighting for chips. Why should I stay here with them?' He said all this while still looking out the window.

Mariam couldn't help seeing it from Alem's point of view. 'Yes, you're right. I heard about the fight and it was stupid, and it is difficult to make friends here, but you must understand that every boy here is here because they have problems at home, and some of them have no home at all. Everyone's problems are different. People may seem strange to you, but then you may seem strange to them. You've been hurt in one way, they've been hurt in another way.'

Alem picked up his bag and put it in his lap. 'I know, you're right, but I still don't like it here.'

'All right,' Mariam said, raising her tone. 'You see that lady I came here with? That's Sheila, she's a social worker and she is here to help you. We – the Refugee Council – are a support group really, but she has connections, so she can really help you. What she said she could do is to fix you up with foster parents. She's been working on it since yesterday and she already has a family for you to see.'

'What is foster parent?' Alem asked.

'Foster parents are people who will take you into their home for a short time or even a long time. It's not a home like this; you'll be living in a normal house with a family. Sheila will explain more.'

Mariam called Sheila in. She was well dressed and from the West Country. In her well-spoken way she explained to Alem that the family she had in mind knew about him and were willing to take him on for as long as necessary but that it was important that he would get on with the family.

Things were moving so fast that Alem was finding it hard to keep up, but he was sure that he didn't want to stay in the children's home and he could see no other option. He agreed to see the family and within minutes he was being taken from the children's home.

Alem sat at the back of Mariam's old Volkswagen and Sheila sat in the front passenger seat. As they drove towards London, Sheila would turn awkwardly in order to speak to Alem. It was mainly small talk until she quietly announced, 'I'm afraid we have a little bit of bad news, it's not the end of the world but it means we have to stop off for a while.'

'What is the matter?' Alem asked glancing from Sheila to the back of Mariam's head and back to Sheila.

Mariam stayed silent. Sheila continued, 'I'm afraid we have to stop off at the Home Office in Croydon for a screening. It's something we have to do but it shouldn't take too long.'

Alem was very casual about it but he could sense Sheila's nervousness. 'What is screening?'

'In a screening they take photos of you and they also do other things to make sure they know who you are. The government requires all asylum seekers to go through it now.'

'It's not very nice,' Mariam said, without taking her eyes of the road.

Just after an hour they were at the Home Office in Croydon, and after waiting for half an hour Alem went in for the screening, with Sheila and Mariam closely watching every detail. Alem was photographed, fingerprinted, interviewed and given a number. On the way out he was given a piece of paper, which he had to sign to confirm his number.

Alem was humiliated by the process. As they drove deeper into London, Alem asked if he was now a criminal, to which Mariam replied, 'The system is not fair. There is no one more innocent than you, but look at the way you've been treated. Criminals are all over the world but the big difference between a dictatorship and a democracy is that in a democracy the criminals are voted in.'

There was bitterness in Mariam's voice, as watching the screening process had brought back memories of her own screening. She had to tell herself to stop talking; she didn't want to bombard Alem with her personal views. So, they continued the journey with Alem staring down at his hands, which were still stained with the ink from the fingerprinting session.

CHAPTER 8

~ The Family's Fine ~

They arrived in the late afternoon at a house in an area known as Manor Park to the east of the city. Here he met Mr and Mrs Fitzgerald and Ruth, their only child, who was seventeen years old. Ruth had long black hair that she let hang halfway down her back and a slim face with brown eyes. She worked as a sales assistant in an electrical shop. Mr and Mrs Fitzgerald were born in Ireland but Ruth was born in Manor Park.

Mrs Fitzgerald had completely lost her accent and now sounded like an older version of Ruth. As she spoke to Alem, she used a yellow cloth and dusted anything that came within arm's reach. 'Nice to see you, dear, we've heard a lot about you and you're welcome here. It's not much, but it's ours. We're not rich, but we don't starve,' she said, leading them into the front room.

They occupied a three-bedroom house on Meanly Road where Mr and Mrs Fitzgerald had lived since getting married in 1977 when they were both just eighteen years old.

Alem was surprised at how comfortable he felt with the family. Mrs Fitzgerald told him that they had fostered many children in the past, some of whom were teenagers from various parts of the world. Mr Fitzgerald didn't say much but they very quickly made Alem feel at home without pampering him or seeming condescending. The room that was to become Alem's was built as an upstairs extension at the back of the house. It had its own television and a computer, and a large collection of books which immediately caught Alem's attention. So far he had only seen the inside of museums, restaurants, the hotel, the children's home and the barn. This was his first look into a British home. It was warm and he liked it.

There was no formal interview. The family sat with Sheila, Mariam and Alem. They just talked, mainly about other boys and girls that the Fitzgeralds had fostered in the past, but also about the area, the local schools and the increase in cars now parked on the road. Alem was offered lots of cups of tea and he refused them all, but he ate every biscuit in sight, while Sheila and Mariam drank every cup of tea that came their way.

As he ate, Alem observed Mr and Mrs Fitzgerald. Mr Fitzgerald had a shaven face but was going bald. He still had traces of an Irish accent and was a short, round sort of a man with a belly that made him look as if he was about to give birth. Mrs Fitzgerald was of

86

a similar height to her husband but without the belly, and was a lot more alert than he was. Mrs Fitzgerald explained that her husband had taken early retirement from his electrician job and spent most of his time whispering to the fifteen fish that he kept in the garden. Mr Fitzgerald sat nodding in agreement saying 'Yes' and 'That's right' periodically. It occurred to Alem that if he didn't know that they were husband and wife, he could have taken them for brother and sister.

After the visit to the house, Sheila and Mariam took Alem to the local Social Services offices, where he was asked the big question: 'Do you want to stay there?'

'What choice do I have?' Alem asked Sheila.

'Well, there are other families and there are other children's homes. We know you don't like children's homes, and I have checked out the possibility of you seeing other families, but they would take time to sort out. The good thing about this family is that you can move in tonight; all I have to do is sign some papers. But it's up to you.'

Alem quickly sensed that things could be much worse and that he was on to a good thing. 'I want to stay with this family,' he said.

'Great,' Sheila replied. 'I really do think you will get on fine there. I've known the Fitzgeralds for ages and they've never let us down yet. And look, Alem, you don't have to stay a day longer than you want to. If you feel that things aren't going well, we'll think again, and we will keep reviewing your situation anyway. If there are any problems, all you have to do is tell me or Mariam, and we will try our best to help you out.'

Alem was happy to have succeeded in getting out of the children's home, but he couldn't help thinking about the bigger picture. 'How long will I be staying here for?' he asked.

'No one can say, Alem. We could trace members of your family tomorrow.'

'I haven't got any family here,' Alem interrupted quickly.

'OK, but your parents could turn up tomorrow, or the fighting could stop tomorrow; we just don't know. First of all we must make sure that you're safe and secure, then we will look further into your case.'

Early that evening Alem was taken back to the Fitzgeralds' household, where he received a lively welcome from Mr and Mrs Fitzgerald but a more cautious one from Ruth.

Alem spent the first two weeks doing nothing but watching television and reading books. Mr Fitzgerald hardly ever left the house, except to go to the shops with Mrs Fitzgerald. Ruth didn't talk to him much;

she spent most of her time in her room listening to Brit-pop bands complaining about love and the system, or patrolling the streets with her girl gang. Alem could sense a deep unhappiness about her.

He would get quietly excited when he walked the streets and saw other Ethiopians and Eritreans. He could identify East Africans easily but they didn't seem to acknowledge him in any way. It didn't take long for him to realise that this was not malicious, it was simply the way that people lived in London; everybody was minding their own business. There were many Africans and he would go nowhere and do nothing if he was to have a conversation with every one that he saw.

He was slowly getting used to the food, but he didn't find it inspiring. It was very much the meat-and-two-veg type, but the Fitzgeralds did experiment sometimes and gravy was always available to make the food wet. He was bought warm clothes with the financial allowance that was given for him. Sheila phoned regularly and visited them twice, and on one occasion she brought Mariam along with her. Alem was doing fine but he did lack one crucial thing, which he brought to the attention of the Fitzgeralds over the remains of an evening meal.

'Do you think that it's possible for me to go to school here?'

'Of course,' replied Mrs Fitzgerald. 'In fact, I did

have a word with Sheila about that and she said that she had already spoken to the local school and that we should apply when you have settled in. We can go any time, they're expecting us.'

'I have settled in,' Alem said gleefully.

'You can say that again,' said Mr Fitzgerald, nodding in the direction of Alem's empty plate. 'Now would you like a cup of tea?'

'No, thanks.'

'Biscuits?'

'Yes, please.' Alem had developed a strong liking for biscuits, especially the Bourbon type, but he wasn't keen on tea.

Ruth picked seedless grapes from a large bunch on the table in the dining room. Alem stretched his arm out, holding the plate of biscuits in her direction.

'Would you like a biscuit, Ruth?'

'No,' she said, staring into the grapes.

He asked another question in an attempt to strike up a conversation. 'Do you like biscuits?'

'Sometimes.'

'In Africa we have very strong thick coffee, do you have that here?'

'I don't know,' Ruth replied.

'What I have noticed in England is that so many people drink tea; everywhere you go, people ask if you want a cup of tea. We have tea back home but here people drink it every five minutes, and tea here is so full of milk.'

'So what?' Ruth answered abruptly. She stood up and stormed out of the dining room.

Mrs Fitzgerald shouted, 'Ruth, you come back here now!'

Ruth walked slowly back into the room. 'What's wrong now?'

'You know what's wrong,' Mrs Fitzgerald said. 'Why are you speaking to Alem like that?'

'Like what?'

'Like that, all rude and abrupt. Have some manners!'

'I'm not rude and abrupt – anyway I'm not feeling well, I have to go to the bathroom,' she said as she started to walk out.

Mrs Fitzgerald turned to Alem. 'I'm sorry, sometimes she gets like this. It's nothing, just ignore her.'

There were no more such outbursts but the tension was ever present. And there was not much for them to talk about. Ruth was into pop music, Alem was into books; Alem loved buildings, Ruth loved clothes; Alem thought Ruth's parents were interesting, Ruth thought they were boring; Alem was thirsty for knowledge but Ruth thought that she knew it all.

Despite the lack of communication between him and Ruth, Alem did not have a single bad word to say against the Fitzgerald family – at one point he even tried hard to find faults after watching a television programme on the failures of mixed-race adoption. The programme highlighted case after case of white families that had adopted and fostered black kids and failed because of a lack of understanding or of cultural differences. But Alem was sure the Ruth problem wasn't about race, and he had come to the conclusion that the Fitzgerald family's willingness to look after him was more important than their lack of African culture. Their lack of African culture was not their fault.

The day before Alem had to visit the school, Mrs Fitzgerald called Ruth into the living room where Alem was sitting. 'Ruth, tell Alem about the school! It wasn't that long ago you were there, I suspect not much has changed.'

Ruth sat on the chair opposite Alem. She sighed and crossed her legs and began to pick things off her jeans that could only have been visible to her eyes. Her mother noticed her actions, as did Alem.

'Well, the school's called Great Milford,' Ruth said as she groomed her jeans, 'there are more boys than girls, the playground's big, the library's big, the classes are big, the headmaster talks a lot and the teachers are not bad, and when I was there they boasted that they spoke about twenty languages.'

'What!' Alem said, eyebrows raised high in surprise. 'The teachers are that good, they speak twenty different languages?'

'No,' said Ruth, 'I didn't mean it like that. They – the teachers – were boasting that there were about twenty different languages spoken by the pupils of the school.'

'What else?' Mrs Fitzgerald said. 'Tell him more.'

'The building's about seventy years old, the teachers are about seventy years old, it's never had a royal visit, and there's mice in the kitchen. It's OK, but I hated it,' she said.

Ruth was serious. Alem smiled. Mrs Fitzgerald said, 'I knew I shouldn't have asked you.'

Early the next morning Alem went to the school with Mrs Fitzgerald to make enquiries about his admission. After an interview with the headmaster, they were told to go home and wait. They were assured that the school would contact them very soon.

That night Alem took longer than usual to fall asleep. He was excited about the prospect of going to school; he missed school and was eager to take up the challenge of learning in an English school. When he had thought enough about that subject, he began to look at the photo and think about his family's situation. Since moving to Manor Park, he had been so busy getting to know the area and getting to know the Fitzgeralds that he hadn't had much time to think about anything else. At quieter moments, when he was not watching television or reading one of the many books in his room, he would be playing CD-ROM games on the computer. He was slow at first but he soon learned how to play games such as Treasure Hunt and Euro Racer. When he was not playing he would be working his way around one of the many educational CD-ROMs.

Alem was amazed at the amount of knowledge that was lying around in his bedroom. When he first moved into the room he formed a plan that he had not told anyone about: he wanted to read every book in his room. But in his overeagerness to learn, he hadn't finished a single one. Instead, at the side of his bed he had four piles of books, each one with a bookmark inside it, each one unfinished. His ambition had changed. All he wanted to do now was to finish one; he only wondered which book he would finish first. His inability to finish a book was not due to laziness, on the contrary, he wanted to know everything immediately, he couldn't learn quickly enough. There were times when he would sit on his bed reading one book, and then he would stop to mentally digest something he had just read. He would spot another book sitting on the shelves waiting for a mind, a bookmark would be placed in the book he was reading, that book would join the queue at the side of his bed, and the newly discovered book would be taken off the shelf. But it would only be a matter of time before the new love would be cast aside, and Alem would go on another literary adventure.

As he lay on his bed in the darkness, he thought about what was happening back home. He wondered how his parents were and what was happening to his friend Dawit back in Ethiopia. Although people knew Alem's story, no one really talked about the war back home; London was like another world. Until now life here had been relatively easy; he had had a scrap in the children's home, he couldn't quite understand Ruth, he hated the cold, but he hadn't seen a gun or heard any aircraft fire. He knew a little about the British Empire, still he couldn't understand how Britain had gained its reputation for being a strong military power because he hadn't seen a single soldier on its streets. Where were these soldiers? He might not have put great effort into keeping up with what was happening with the war back home but not a day passed without him thinking about his parents. It was hard trying to remember his parents and forget the war at the same time.

In the morning a very excited Mrs Fitzgerald shook Alem with one hand – 'Alem, Alem, wake up!' In the other hand she held a spatula. She was wearing a flowery apron and was flushed with excitement. 'Alem, good news! I've just had a phone call from Great Milford. You can start school on Monday. Isn't that just wonderful now?'

'Yes, Mrs Fitzgerald,' Alem replied, excited but a little too sleepy to express his excitement, 'it's just wonderful now. How long can I stay there for?'

'You can stay there for as long as you like,' she said, levelling out her voice. 'You can stay there until you're sixteen if you like, if you're good, that is; it's your school.'

Alem swiftly sat up in the bed. 'What, do you think I will still be here when I am sixteen?'

'That's another question,' Mrs Fitzgerald replied, 'and one we don't know the answer to – so let's deal with what we know now, you're going to school. Come down and get your breakfast, there's a good boy.' She looked down on the floor and then at the bookshelves. 'Alem, Mr Fitzgerald made all these wonderful bookshelves so that the books could be put on them for safekeeping; try using them, please.'

'Yes, Mrs Fitzgerald, I'm sorry,' Alem replied, looking down at the tower blocks of books he had created.

The main topic of conversation at breakfast was the admission of Alem to the school. Alem asked many questions about attending the school, most of which were about money. He found it hard to believe that not only was the attendance at the school free, but he didn't have to pay for books either. Mrs Fitzgerald told Alem that she already had a uniform on order with a deposit paid.

Alem and Mrs Fitzgerald spent most of Saturday shopping on Romford Road. Alem's uniform was ready and waiting for him and it fitted perfectly, but he also had to try on new trainers and get the right bag to put them in. Most of the shopkeepers were familiar with Mrs Fitzgerald. Alem could see that she had done this before, but still he felt special being the centre of attention.

He spent most of Sunday trying on his new uniform.

CHAPTER 9

~ First Class ~

'Those of you who are observant will have noticed that new wastepaper baskets have been placed at various locations around the playground. Personally, I have always felt that the number of bins that we had previously was adequate, but judging by the amount of litter we are finding in the playground, it seems that many of you are unable to use one unless it is right under your nose. I do hope that you will make use of these waste-placement vessels from now on. They do cost money, they do have a purpose, and they do help to make the school a much better place to be in.'

Alem sat right at the back of the assembly hall listening to the headmaster speaking. He had never seen anything like this. Teachers looked on from various points around the hall as the headmaster delivered his address to the fidgety pupils from the raised stage. Alem was mesmerised.

'Unfortunately, two boys were permanently excluded last week for bringing knives on to the school premises. We exclude pupils only very reluctantly from this school, but there are simply no two ways about it, we will *not* tolerate the presence of any weapons on these premises. We, all of us here, sent a message of condolence to St Luke's when Mr Gatsby was stabbed to death in his own classroom. And then, in this very hall, we spoke about what could have possibly led up to such a killing taking place in an educational institution. And all of us agreed – and if I remember well, there were no dissenting voices – that we would try our very best to make sure that we never reached that point. Well, this was the second time those boys had been caught with knives. They simply could not be allowed to get away with it a second time, so I was left with no alternative but to exclude them. Let this be a lesson to you all, but more important, let the death of Mr Gatsby be a lesson to us all. Remember our school motto, *live to learn, learn to live,* and let us be true to our word.'

Alem was still fully focused on the headmaster. He took in every single word as if his life depended on it. He was shocked by what he was hearing and wondered if the headmaster might be exaggerating. This was the first talk of anything like war that he had heard since arriving in Britain and here he was, hearing it on his first day at school.

'Now I want to give you some good news,' the headmaster continued. 'Those of you that read the *Newham Recorder* would have seen two of our pupils on its front page this week. Both Teresa Grant and Inderjit Singh made the front page of our local paper because of the amount of time they have devoted to helping the older members of our community. This is an example of the kind of news that Great Milford School should be known for; these are the kind of pupils that we can all be proud of. I would like them both to come up on the stage to receive one of our very own Positive Pupil's Certificates.'

The two pupils walked to the stage to receive their certificates as the teachers and the other pupils clapped. Alem clapped and quietly whispered to himself, 'Positive pupil.' He liked the sound of it.

'Now, off to your classes, and let's be wiser come the end of the day,' said the headmaster as the two pupils left the stage. Immediately, the hall erupted with sound as everyone stood up and began to chatter.

'Quietly!' shouted the headmaster at the top of his voice.

'Hello, Alem!' The voice came from a teacher approaching him. She was wearing a sari and it looked to Alem as if she was gliding towards him. 'My name is Mrs Kumar, I'm head of your form and I need to give you this.' She handed him a timetable. 'If you spend a few minutes on it, you'll see how it works. Pretty straightforward really, subject, classroom, time, it's easy, and if you have any problems finding the classrooms, just ask another pupil. Your first lesson is

English. I'm going that way, follow me.'

Two corridors later, Mrs Kumar opened the class-room door for Alem. 'There you go,' she said and walked away.

Alem nervously walked into the room. There was no teacher. Pupils were sitting or standing around their desks talking loudly and joking. Alem didn't know what to do with himself. He stood just inside the room waiting for something to happen, hoping that the teacher would come and instruct him on pro-tocol, or at least tell him where to sit. Some of the pupils glanced at Alem but carried on telling their stories and trying to make each other laugh. Alem felt insignificant.

Suddenly a pupil ran into the classroom, swinging open the door with great force. It hit Alem in the back and knocked him to the floor. The whole class began laughing. Alem lay completely still. He was physically unhurt but wished he could disappear through the crack in the floorboard that he was now looking down at. He wanted to fade away and reap-pear back home with the Fitzgeralds.

'To your seats – now!' The powerful shout came from a teacher standing beside Alem. The voice filled the room; the pupils fell silent, leaving the teacher's shout to reverberate around the room for a few seconds.

Alem looked up; the teacher towered above him

like a giant. He leaned down and stretched out a helping hand.

'And what are you doing down there?'

'Getting up,' shouted an unidentifiable pupil.

'That's enough of that.' The teacher helped Alem to his feet. 'What happened here?' he continued.

'I don't know.' Alem's words were barely audible.

'You don't know; why don't you know?'

Alem had nothing new to say. 'I don't know.'

'It was my fault, sir,' a voice interrupted.

'You again, Fern?'

'Sir, I wasn't doing anything wrong. I was running to get to the lesson, and when I opened the door, the door hit him and he fell to the floor. It was an accident, sir, I didn't mean it – honest, sir.'

'Is this true?' the teacher said, looking towards Alem.

'I don't know,' Alem said completely sincerely.

All the pupils burst into laughter once more.

'Quiet!' the teacher shouted loudly. He put his hands on his hips and growled at Alem in a feeble attempt to look hard. 'Do you know any other words?'

'I don't know.' Alem hesitated. There were sniggers as the pupils tried hard to hold back and not laugh out loud.

Alem was confused. 'No – I mean yes – I mean I do, yes, I do know some more words.'

'Good,' said the teacher, sensing a conclusion. 'Is his version of events true?'

'Yes,' Alem said loud and clear.

'OK, that's all I wanted to know. Now, both of you, to your seats – and Fern, don't run in the building, and watch where you're going or you'll end up on the floor and you'll be lost for words.'

The boy walked away. Alem looked at the teacher, not knowing what to do with himself. 'Please, teacher, where do I sit?'

'On a chair,' shouted another voice.

There was more laughter from the class.

'Quiet, please,' said the teacher. 'Wherever you can find a seat,' he said, looking around the classroom.

From the back of the room the boy who had just knocked Alem down spoke. 'He could sit next to me, sir,' he said, pointing to the empty seat next to him.

'Would you like to sit there?' the teacher asked, unsure whether Alem would want to sit next to the boy who had just floored him.

'Yes,' Alem replied, tactfully adding 'sir' in imitation of the other boy addressing the teacher.

Alem was pleased to be going to the back of the class. After his big entrance, all he wanted to do now was sink into the background. But that was not to happen; he was to be the centre of attention for a little longer.

'You must be the new boy,' the teacher said to

Alem. Now the whole class turned to look at Alem again.

'Yes, sir.'

'And your name?'

'Alem Kelo.'

'Well, my name is Mr Walsh and I'm sure you'll get to know the rest of the class soon enough. Have you ever read Charles Dickens, Alem?'

'No, but I have heard of him,' said Alem enthusiastically.

'Very good,' said the teacher. 'We have all read *Great Expectations*, and today I would like us to discuss some of the issues raised in the novel. So for now you can just listen, but if you would like to make a contribution to the debate, feel free to do so.'

The pupils turned to face the teacher and the lesson started. Although Alem had not read *Great Expectations*, there were plenty of times when he wanted to join in the debate but he just didn't want to attract any kind of attention to himself.

Outside the classroom after the lesson the boy who had knocked Alem down went straight to him.

'Sorry about that, mate, I really didn't mean it. I thought I was late for the lesson so there's me running through the school like a nutter and there you was behind the door. Sorry.'

'It is OK, I was not hurt,' Alem replied smiling.

'So yu new then?'

104

'Yes, my first day and now I shall never forget my first entrance into an English classroom.'

'I said I'm sorry,' the boy replied swiftly.

'No, it's OK, maybe in the future I will think it was quite funny – it's possible.'

'My name's Robert. Have you got science now?'

Alem pulled out the timetable from his bag and looked at it. 'Yes.'

'Me too,' Robert replied, walking away quickly. 'Let's go.'

There were no major problems throughout the rest of the day. Alem's approach to the lessons was pretty much the same: take it easy, look, listen and pick up what you can. The teachers were aware that Alem was starting in the middle of the school term and most soon realised that he was new to the country.

At dinnertime Robert found Alem wandering in the playground and invited him out to the fish and chip shop. They joined the queue and after a wait of about fifteen minutes, they managed to get themselves a bag of chips each. Alem had developed a habit of reading every notice in sight and was amused by the notice on the outside door of the shop. It said: 'Only 3 schoolchildren at any one time.'

After eating their chips they went on to the newsagent's to buy some chocolates and there he saw a similar sign: 'No more than 3 schoolchildren allowed.'

Alem had read about the English tradition of queuing, but after spending most of his dinnertime waiting in line, he couldn't understand why these shopkeepers were so keen on preserving this tradition and making them queue outside their shops for as long as possible.

Alem and Robert were sitting on a wall finishing their chocolates when Robert looked at his watch. 'Only ten minutes left, guy,' he shouted, alluding to some type of emergency. He reached for the inside pocket of his jacket and pulled out a packet of cigarettes. 'Want a fag?'

Alem was horrified. 'Do you smoke?' he said, shaking his head vigorously.

'Yeah, so do you want one or what?'

'No,' Alem replied calmly, 'I'm much too young to smoke and look how close you are to school.'

'Loads of kids smoke, look.'

Alem looked around and noticed that many of the pupils were smoking, some even while heading back towards the school.

'Is this allowed?' he said, surprised.

'They can't stop us,' Robert said smugly. 'What can they do? So long as you put it out before you enter the school gates, you're OK. You see that girl there?' he said, pointing his cigarette in the direction of a girl walking towards them. 'Look, she's smoking, she smokes like a factory, and her dad's a teacher, so don't fret, guy, yu safe, trust me.' He held the cigarette packet out, inviting Alem to partake.

'No, it's OK,' Alem said, pulling out his timetable to indicate his lack of interest.

At the end of the day the smokers were more obvious. Alem found that as soon as they left the school grounds, many pupils lit cigarettes and few made any attempt to hide them. One boy even waved to a teacher who was leaving the school in his car.

Alem made his way home alone. There was a spring in his step. All things considered, he thought it had been an interesting, if not perfect, first day in school. When he got to the road where he lived, he ran the rest of the way. He rang the bell and knocked on the door. Mrs Fitzgerald opened the door and Alem bounced in, a little out of breath but excited.

'Mrs Fitzgerald, school was so good! So many different students, so many different lessons, and every lesson was in a different classroom.'

'So you liked it then?' Mrs Fitzgerald gave him a warm, motherly smile.

'Yes. I made a few mistakes and I got pushed over flat on the ground, but that was an accident. It's good, I liked it.'

'And you want to go back?' she asked, heading for the kitchen with Alem trailing behind her.

'Of course I do!'

'Very good. Now, Alem, I want you to go up to

your room, put your things away and change your clothes. The lady from the refugee place rang earlier, she wants to see you. She said she'd be here soon. Hurry up now.'

Alem looked puzzled. 'What does she want to see me for?'

'I don't honestly know, but don't worry. I asked her the very same question and she told me not to worry. She said it looked like good news.'

An hour later Mariam arrived at the house. Mr Fitzgerald joined them in the living room, knowing that something was going to happen.

Mariam looked Alem up and down as if he was a relative she hadn't seen for years. 'You look very well, Alem. How was school?'

'All right, thank you.'

'Did you make any friends?'

'I spoke to many people and made one friend.'

'That's not bad,' Mariam said.

'Please, please sit down,' Mr Fitzgerald interjected. They all found themselves seats.

Mariam continued with her small talk. 'When I first went to school it took me a whole week before I made any friends. It was terrible; things got better but it took time.'

'Cup of tea?' Mrs Fitzgerald asked and everyone except Alem nodded their heads eagerly.

Once the tea was on the table, Mariam revealed her reason for coming. When she spoke, she addressed Alem as if no one else was in the room.

'Well, Alem, as you know, your application for political asylum has been submitted and we are still waiting for a response from the Home Office. We know that you said you didn't have any relatives in Britain but we still made some investigations just in case there were some that you didn't know about, and we have had no luck there.'

Alem couldn't understand why she should doubt him. 'I told you that I have no relatives here. What's the matter? Don't you believe me?'

'I believe you,' Mariam replied, trying to reassure him, 'but it's not just about me; besides, we've had cases in the past where some asylum seekers genuinely were not aware they had relatives here.'

'If I had relatives here, I would find them myself,' Alem said slowly and firmly. Mariam knew he meant it.

She put her file on her lap and began scrabbling through it, speaking as she did so. 'This arrived yesterday at our head office in London.' She pulled out a blue airmail letter; she leaned forward to hand it over to Alem. 'It's addressed to you, we have not opened it.'

Alem took one look at it and immediately sprang off his seat. 'It's from my father, I can see! It's from my father, I know it! I know his writing! Oh, Mariam, I am so happy! Mrs Fitzgerald, it's my father!'

For a few moments Alem walked in circles around his chair, looking at the letter as if it was a winning lottery ticket which was just about to change his life. The letter was a breakthrough. Everyone else looked at each other and smiled, pleased that Alem was pleased.

Alem sat down and began to open the letter. It was an awkward letter to open. It was one of those extra-light airmail letters that fold in such a way that the letter itself becomes the envelope.

'I've a letter opener,' Mr Fitzgerald said, turning to leave the room.

'Actually,' Mariam interrupted swiftly, 'I think it may be best if you read the letter alone, Alem.'

Alem stopped. The room went silent as he looked around for a reaction.

'Go to your room if you like, it's probably best if you read it in your own space,' Mrs Fitzgerald said.

Alem headed upstairs and Mrs Fitzgerald began to pour Mariam more tea. 'How would his father know how to contact him?' she enquired.

'The Refugee Council is well known around the world, and many people know that if someone is in Britain and they are in the process of seeking refugee status, we can usually track them down.'

'Tell me something,' Mr Fitzgerald said, eager to learn, 'are there British refugees in other countries?'

'Oh, yes,' Mariam replied. 'You would be surprised how many British refugees there are in places like Brazil and Mexico. They're usually whistle blowers but there are very old political refugees from the time of World War II still living in Russia and Cuba.'

For the next fifteen minutes they drank more tea and talked about Cuba. Then it occurred to Mariam that they had heard nothing from Alem, so she expressed her concern to Mrs Fitzgerald, who went up to his room and stood outside the door.

'Alem?' she said, but there was no reply. 'Alem, are you all right?'

There was still no reply. She knocked on the door and raised her voice. 'Alem, is anything the matter?'

Mariam heard the calls and went and stood at the bottom of the stairs. 'Is everything all right, Mrs Fitzgerald?'

'I don't know,' she replied, 'Alem's not answering me. Alem,' she continued, 'Alem, can I come in?'

At last Alem replied. His voice was quiet, conveying no obvious emotion. 'No, please don't come in. I'm OK – I shall come down soon. Please leave me alone for a while, I will be down soon.'

'As you say,' said Mrs Fitzgerald, and she made her way downstairs.

Back in the living room Mrs Fitzgerald told Mariam what Alem had said and then offered her another cup of tea.

Nobody knew what to think or do. The tea ritual was now useful because it meant that something was happening in the room. Then as they drank, they heard Alem making his way slowly down the stairs. He entered the room expressionless. He sat back in the seat where he sat previously and threw the letter on the coffee table in the centre of the room. It slid across the table and ended up tucked under the saucer of Mariam's cup.

'Read it, Mariam, and then tell me what I should do,' Alem said.

Mariam picked up the letter, unfolded it and read it silently to herself. The only sound that could be heard was the sound of rush-hour traffic and barking dogs in the distance.

My dearest son,

I do hope this letter finds you soon and that you are as well as can be. War is such a terrible thing, my son, I hope you never witness it again. Darkness is upon our land; it seems that every man that is alive is limping and that there are bloodstains on the dresses of all our women. Today I found the arm of a man lying at the side of a street. No body, just one arm. And I found myself asking trivial questions like, 'Is this an Ethiopian or an Eritrean arm?' Could you believe it? I was asking this question, I, the great Pan-Africanist. War is eating away at our souls, young man, it is terrible.

Sadly I must tell you that I have bad news. From the day I returned here I have been searching but I cannot find your mother. She left your auntie's house in Asmara to go visit your grandmother in Badme. Some people tell me she has been seen in Ethiopia, some say she is in Eritrea, but I have tried everywhere I can think of and I can't find her. When I came back I found that your auntie's house had been looted and burnt but your auntie got out in time. She is with your grandmother now. It has been very hard for me. I have hardly slept since I came back here. I did not want to give you such news but what can I do? You must know the truth, son. I can't find your mother. I ask myself, what kind of a place do I live in if I can't find your mother, my wife and our love? But I can casually find the arm of someone I don't know just lying in the streets.

The organisation of EAST has fallen apart and now there is not a single organisation working for peace in the region. It seems that our people are so busy dealing with war that there is no time to deal in peace. Our Eritrean office has been raided and our Ethiopian office has been raided too. It is so sad that our only surviving branch is in London.

I hope you understand why we had to leave you in England for a while. I have so much work to do, and I will not stop until I find your mother. Be strong, young man. Learn more English and remember to love your neighbour. I will write you another letter soon.

Your loving father

Mariam carefully folded the letter. 'Your father said be strong and that's exactly what you must be,' she said, placing the letter on the table.

The front door opened. It was Ruth returning from work. 'Hello, I'm home,' she shouted, running upstairs to play some CDs.

Mr and Mrs Fitzgerald sat awkwardly looking at each other, trying not to catch the eyes of Mariam or Alem. As always, the first to speak up was Mrs Fitzgerald.

'So what is it? Can we help?'

'Alem will explain when he is ready,' Mariam said.

'I am ready,' Alem said. 'You can read the letter,' he said, looking at Mrs Fitzgerald.

Mrs Fitzgerald began to feel it was unwise to push for too much information. She decided to back off. 'It's all right, tell us about it later.'

But Alem could see no reason why it had to be left until later. He leaned forward, picked up the letter and handed it to Mrs Fitzgerald. As he leaned back, he announced, 'My mother is gone.'

The Fitzgeralds simultaneously broke out into speech.

'What do you mean she's gone? There must be some mistake,' said Mrs Fitzgerald.

'Gone where?' asked Mr Fitzgerald.

Alem fixed his gaze on the coffee table. 'Nobody knows. She might be kidnapped, or soldiers could have made her into a slave.'

'Oh, god, oh, my god! That's a terrible thought,' said Mr Fitzgerald, closing his eyes and shaking his head.

Mariam raised her voice, making sure everyone else heard her. 'No, Alem, that is not what the letter says, and you must not assume such things.'

'So where is my mother?' Alem asked, looking straight into Mariam's eyes. 'These are the kinds of things that soldiers do.'

'We don't know what's happened,' Mariam replied, raising her shoulders and stretching the upturned palms of her hands towards Alem as if to invite suggestions. 'But because your father has had problems finding her, you don't have to assume the worst. He may have found her even before this letter arrived. He will write again soon and, who knows, your next letter may be written by her, we just don't know.'

Alem stood up. 'I must go to my room.'

'Don't worry, Alem,' Mariam said, trying to reassure him.

Alem's mood remained unchanged. He still showed little emotion. Nobody had seen him as cold as this before. Once more he looked directly into the eyes of Mariam as he spoke.

'You are an African, Mariam, you know Eritrea, you know Ethiopia, and you also know that where we come from, when a woman disappears, anything is possible. They are burning down houses, they are bombing schools, there are pieces of people's bodies lying in the streets; this is war, and war is bad wherever it is. But the war that is happening in Eritrea and Ethiopia is so cruel. It is like a family at war, it is neighbour killing neighbour. We are killing ourselves as if we never want to see ourselves again, and when you hate yourself this much, anything is possible.'

The Fitzgeralds saw Mariam shudder from the truth and drop her head in silence.

Mrs Fitzgerald stood up, put the letter on the table, rubbed her hands together and said, 'I think I'll go and make some fresh tea.'

CHAPTER 10

~ What the Papers Say ~

Alem hated the idea of becoming some kind of problem to the Fitzgerald family, so he did his best not to inconvenience them in any way and he tried to continue life as normal. Even on the very evening that he received the news about his mother's disappearance, he still ate his evening meal with them and he remained his well-mannered self. Still he was convinced that his mother was being used as some kind of slave or being kept prisoner. For a moment he wondered who could be responsible, but that mattered very little to him; they were Africans, they were human beings.

He read the letter countless times that night, trying to pluck clues from every line. If the house has been burnt and looted, where was my father living? And why did my father not put a return address on the letter?

EAST stood for the East African Solidarity Trust, an organisation dedicated to unifying the various tribes of the region. Alem's parents were both involved with it, but Alem had had no idea that they had an office in London. Now he wondered where that office was.

Although he had only managed to sleep for a couple of hours, the next morning Alem was awake early. He found a copy of *Great Expectations* on his bookshelf and he read the first chapter before he went down to breakfast.

Ruth played her music as always but Mr and Mrs Fitzgerald had been very quiet the night before and they were the same the next morning. It bothered Alem, he felt that he had caused the atmosphere of the household to change, but he knew that there was nothing much that he could do. The night before, the Fitzgeralds had had a quiet family meeting while Alem was in his room. Ruth was a reluctant participant in the meeting – she would have much preferred to be somewhere else. She was warned by her mother to be more considerate to Alem. Mr and Mrs Fitzgerald had decided that they had to go as softly as they could with him, avoiding references to his homeland and giving him as much space as he needed. But what Alem wanted was normality. When Mrs Fitzgerald told Alem that it wouldn't be taken badly if he missed school, Alem insisted on going.

So a determined Alem attended school for the second time. While he was at school, Mrs Fitzgerald rang Sheila the social worker to explain what had happened. Sheila already knew about the letter, Mariam had got to her first, but like the Fitzgeralds she was surprised that Alem had gone to school that day. Sheila's instinct was to pay the family a visit but having heard about Alem's reaction to the letter, she thought it best to leave him alone for a little while longer. Mrs Fitzgerald thought that in many respects Alem was handling the situation quite well. He did not shout, he hadn't torn anything up, he hadn't kicked anything down. His self-control impressed Mrs Fitzgerald but it worried Sheila.

'He's carrying unopened baggage,' she said in a caring-social-worker kind of way. 'Soon he will have to open the baggage and deal with the contents.'

'What do you mean?' Mrs Fitzgerald asked, dropping her voice as if Alem could hear from school.

'He's like a time bomb waiting to go off.'

'Are you sure?' Mrs Fitzgerald asked, wondering whether Sheila had lost her own baggage altogether.

'Yes, he's bottling it all up, and one day he may explode emotionally. He can cope with the stuff in his cup now, but one day his cup will runneth over.'

'Oh,' Mrs Fitzgerald said, a little puzzled by Sheila's use of metaphors. 'So when do you think his cup will runneth over? I mean, do you think he will explode this week?'

'We don't know,' Sheila replied, 'it could be tomorrow, it could be the next day, it could be next year, we just don't know. Some children keep things bottled up all their lives until they are fully grown adults before they deal with it.'

Meanwhile in school Alem was looking, listening and learning. Alongside the exercise books that he was accumulating for the lessons, he had an extra notebook where he wrote down words or phrases that he didn't understand. He would try to understand everything. At dinnertime he met up with Robert again. Robert offered him another cigarette and Alem refused. But he also began to speak to other pupils; struggling to remember the strange names of both the pupils and the teachers, every time he heard a new name he repeated it to himself a few times. Sometimes he would repeat the name until he was out of the person's sight, then he would write it down in his notebook.

Alem smiled very little on his second day at school. He tried not to draw any attention to himself and to be as polite and well behaved as he possibly could. Robert noticed his seriousness. At the school gates, just before departing for their homes, Robert tried to find out what was on Alem's mind.

'What's the matter? Don't you like the school or what?' he asked playfully.

'I like the school very much,' Alem replied. 'It is very good, it is full with possibilities. I think the facilities are good, the building is structurally sound, and I think that the students here have a great opportunity to advance, physically, intellectually and socially.'

'Hold on, guy! It may be good but it's not that good,' Robert said, even more playful. 'We got some OK teachers and some OK girls and then there's me, but that don't make it like some kinda posh university or something. A couple of years ago, when I first came here, we were at the bottom of the league table.'

Alem was thrown into confusion. He wasn't sure if he should be taking Robert seriously, but he felt that there was some truth in what he was saying.

'What is a league table?' Alem asked.

'The league table is like a football league. The best schools in the country are on the top and the worst are on the bottom; we were way down near the bottom.'

'What, you have to play all the other schools in the country in some kind of competition?' Alem asked, still confused.

'No, inspectors come round and give us marks or something like that. I don't know, they test the teachers or something. Anyway, don't worry. Once we were somewhere near the bottom, now we're in the middle, maybe even going up, but we ain't all that good. Where do you live anyway?'

'Meanly Road,' Alem replied.

'Meanly Road,' Robert replied, 'I know that road. Maybe over the weekend we could play football. Do you play football?'

'Not really.'

'You don't play football? It's easy. You just kick the ball, do a bit of dribbling and try and get it in the net.'

'I know how to play it, but the question you asked was do I play it – and I don't.'

'So what are you, a professor or something? OK, can you play Rip Speed?'

'What is Rip Speed?'

'It's a computer game, a car-chase game?'

'No,' Alem replied. 'But I can play Euro Racer, that's a car game.'

'OK, now we're talking – do you like girls then?' Robert asked in a bid to take the conversation to another level.

'I have nothing against them,' Alem replied diplomatically.

'I don't believe you, guy. So what do you do in your spare time?' he asked in a last effort to see if they had anything in common.

'I read,' said Alem.

'You read?' Robert said in a mild state of shock. 'Reading is what you do in school, reading is what you do when you're told to. So what do you do when you are not reading, then?'

'I think,' Alem replied.

'See you later,' Robert said, shaking his head as he began to walk away.

For the next couple of days life at home and at school went on without any major incidents. In the house the letter from Alem's father was not mentioned but it was obvious that it was on everybody's mind. Ruth worked and played and managed to tolerate Alem without being openly hostile to him. Mr Fitzgerald continued to watch over his fish in the garden. Mrs Fitzgerald continued to imitate her mother's attempts to maintain a perfectly clean house, where all the meals were on time and the toilet paper never ran out in the holder.

At school Alem had made another friend. His name was Ray Buckley, but his friends called him Buck. Buck was in the same year group as Alem but in a different class. He was tall and slim and looked a bit like a young Mick Jagger. Buck spent most of his spare time playing his guitar. He came from a well-to-do family that had lived in the area for as far back as they could trace, but all he wanted to do was leave the area. He had long slim fingers that looked as if they were designed for the job of playing the guitar, and he had a great love of singer-songwriters, most of whom were no longer walking the earth: John Lennon, Bob Marley and Kurt Cobain were among his favourites. Other kids at school thought that he looked older than his age because of his constant worrying about the state of the world, but he had a kind of wisdom about him which attracted Alem. He smiled very little and was generally thought of as a bit depressive.

Generally speaking Alem liked the quieter kids at school. He couldn't understand why kids who had the opportunity of going to school would want to go into a classroom and make a lot of noise and not learn. Least of all could he understand why some kids would play truant when they had the privilege of going to school. School was preparation for the future, as far as Alem was concerned, and he had no intention of going into the future unprepared.

By the end of the week Alem felt that he had done well and he was already looking forward to the next week. He had offers from Robert and Buck to hang out over the weekend but he declined them all. His plan was to go home and finish *Great Expectations* so that he could be more involved in his English class.

On Friday when he arrived home Mrs Fitzgerald opened the door as always, but Alem could sense that something was not right. She smiled as she said 'Hello' but it wasn't the warm, maternal smile that usually greeted him. Alem wanted to get straight down to it.

'What is the problem, Mrs Fitzgerald?' he asked.

'Mariam from the Refugee Council is here,' she said, pointing to the living room. 'She needs to speak to you.'

Alem entered the room to find Mr Fitzgerald sitting quietly and Mariam drinking tea and eating biscuits.

Mariam stood up. 'Hello, Alem,' she said, smiling.

Alem would not risk smiling, he was aware that what was coming next might not be anything to smile about.

Mrs Fitzgerald entered the room and they all sat down.

'Don't worry,' Mariam said, 'we have a problem but we think we can overcome it.'

'What's the problem?' Alem asked, his eyes compelling her to get to the point.

'We received a letter from Croydon.'

'Who's Croydon?' Alem asked.

'Croydon is not a person, it's a district. Do you remember when we went for that horrible screening?'

'Yes,' Alem nodded.

'Well the letter has come from there. They deal with "in country" applications for asylum.'

'What does "in country" mean?' Alem was interrupting her flow but he wanted to make sure that he understood everything that was said.

'An "in country" application is made by someone who applies for asylum when they are already in the country. The other type is a "port application", that is when someone applies at an airport or a seaport or any kind of entry point. Their applications are taken

125

up by immigration control. Anyway, unfortunately, the Home Office at Croydon has refused your asylum request.'

'What does that mean?' Alem asked, looking around the room as if to invite anyone to answer.

'It means that for some reason they are not happy with your application,' Mariam replied, 'but there is still hope. We can appeal. It will mean, though, that your case will be heard in a small courtroom, with a judge.'

Alem had lots of questions to ask and he couldn't ask them quickly enough.

Alem: Were you expecting this?

Mariam: No, it doesn't happen that often with people of your age.

Alem: Who is this judge?

Mariam: We don't know yet. Some are less reasonable than others. We just don't know. And actually, Alem, they're called *adjudicators*. Same thing really.

Alem: Will they ask me lots of questions?

Mariam: They probably will, but you mustn't let that worry you. We will talk to you more about that later.

Alem: Will I be in the courtroom on my own?

Mariam: No, we will get an immigration solicitor to represent you.

Alem: Can Mr and Mrs Fitzgerald be there?

Mariam: Of course they can.

Alem: Will there be any soldiers there?

Mariam: No way.

Alem: Can they send me back to the war?

Mariam: We think that's very unlikely, but they can.

Alem: Can they send me to jail?

Mariam: We used to think that was impossible, but look.

She handed him a folder that he opened. It contained a wad of newspaper cuttings.

'Those are just from some of today's papers,' Mariam said, leaning back in her seat. 'Read them.'

Alem glanced at the cuttings. The headlines jumped out at him one after the other: 'Government to clamp down on asylum seekers', 'Gypsies, tramps and thieves', 'Refugee beggars flood London streets', 'Government plan to build new detention centre for "bogus" refugees', 'Opposition party propose prison ship for asylum seekers', '57 asylum seekers found dead in container at Dover'.

'What is all this about?' Alem asked.

'Me and my husband are Irish,' Mrs Fitzgerald replied. 'We weren't born here, you know. I came here when I was nine; my mother and father were starving. This country has helped us, this country has a lot to offer. But sometimes the newspapers and the politicians will pick on people to show how powerful they are and make us forget about the real problems. Get the Irish out, stop the travellers, stop the gays, blame the nurses and blame the teachers. They do it all the time. Now it's "get the refugees out".'

Mr Fitzgerald made one of his rare interruptions. 'That's right, boy. There was a time when we had to be careful just because we were Irish. We were treated as if we were all members of the IRA. And I tell you no lie, not so long ago anyone who had any ideas of their own were called loony left or communist, and if you believed most of those so-called newspapers, all the ills in the country were caused by them. Now they want to tell us that the blacks and the refugees are causing all our problems. The truth is that the number of people that leave this country each year is much higher than the number of people that come here. And you know, if people didn't come from abroad, we wouldn't have a health service, or a bus service, and most of the great British corner shops would be gone. And guess what, mate – don't just take it from me, check up on it – even the royal family, yes, even that lot, they came from abroad. These politicians make me sick!'

Mariam was taken aback by his diatribe. 'There's a lot of politics behind these headlines,' she said, pointing to the newspaper cuttings. 'I just thought you should know about the political climate here at the moment. But we have to focus on your case. You'll have a very good barrister, Sheila will be writing a report about you, and the Refugee council will be backing you one hundred per cent.'

'When will this hearing be?' Alem asked.

'We don't have a date yet but it looks like it will be sometime in January. So let us do what has to be done for now and you can get on with school and enjoy your first English Christmas.'

Alem picked up the newspaper cuttings and put them into the folder. 'Can I keep these?' he said to Mariam.

Mariam was a bit surprised by the question. 'Well yes, I suppose so; I can get other copies from the office. But Alem, why do you want to keep them?'

Alem placed the folder on his lap. 'I want to know what these people think of me.'

CHAPTER 11

~ A Way with Words ~

Alem was given the date of 7th of January for the appeal hearing.

For the next few weeks Alem studied hard, even through the half-term break. The first book that he managed to read from cover to cover was *Great Expectations*, and in order to make sure that he could hold his own in any debate on the book, once he had finished reading it he read it again. English was by far his favourite subject, closely followed by design and technology, and science. On the whole there was very little about school that Alem didn't like; each day he entered the school gates hungry for the challenge that lay ahead of him.

At first, he spent much of his break-times in school reading, until he realised that a social life was important too. He also became aware that some of his fellow students saw him as a bit of a nerd, so he began to spend more time hanging out with Robert and Buck. On the whole the teachers and students grew to like Alem; it was difficult not to. He rubbed no one up the wrong way, he worked hard and wasn't threatening to steal anyone's girlfriend. He went to school for an education and he wasn't going to let friendships get in the way. But he did meet his first female redhead at school. She was Christine Kirby. He saw her all the time but they only spoke once in what was a very brief, one-sided conversation outside the school.

She ran towards him as if she was going to run right through him, stopping close enough for him to recognise the flavour of her chewing gum, and said, 'What's your name?'

'Alem Kelo,' Alem replied, thinking that this could be the start of an interesting conversation.

She was in such a hurry, as she replied she chewed and spoke simultaneously. 'Well, Alem, my friend over there fancies you,' she said. Then she ran off.

Alem followed her with his eyes and saw her join a group of four girls looking at him and laughing. And that was it, the ginger-haired girl had come and gone.

Then there were occasions when practical jokes were played on him but he soon learned that it was nothing personal. He became a target because he was new to the school and because he had not familiarised himself with some of the more playful words of the English language.

He had been caught out with word games many times; the most memorable (or the most forgettable, depending on which way you looked at it) was in one particular 'personal, social health education' lesson.

The class was split into small groups to debate a specific subject set by the teacher and on this occasion it was the relationship between church and state. The teacher posed the question, 'Should the government be attached to the church or is religion a personal thing?'

The class broke up into various groups to debate for a short time, after which the groups would reassemble to discuss the topic together. The teacher gave Alem the job of chairing the larger discussion; he thought it would help boost his confidence, and Alem was happy to have been chosen. When the time had come for the main discussion to start, Christopher Stone, a regular joker, moved in.

'Hey, Alem,' he said quite seriously, 'everyone is saying how good the debates have been.'

'That's great,' Alem said, moving into his position in front of the class. 'We should have a very good discussion then.'

'Yes,' said Christopher, sounding excited. 'I chaired one of these once and the teacher likes it if you thank everybody, you know, just thank everybody for taking part in the debates and making them so interesting. And let them know that you are looking forward to the larger debate, we call it a mass debate, you know what "mass" means, don't you?'

'I think so,' Alem said, wondering why he was so concerned about his performance.

'A mass is a large group of people.'

'Yes,' Alem replied, 'I understand.'

Alem stood in front of the class. The teacher nodded his head, signalling that he could now begin. Alem was nervous. He swallowed hard and began.

'The motion we are debating today is the church and state. Is religion political or personal? You have all had the chance to debate the issue in your various groups, I am now looking forward to what should be a very interesting mass debate.'

The class burst into laughter, even the teacher had a smile on his face. It was a trick that had been played before on others but it never failed to get the crowd going. Alem wasn't sure what he had said wrong. He looked towards Christopher for help.

Christopher whispered loudly to him, 'Say you're sorry, you're just a wanker.'

Alem repeated it immediately. 'I'm sorry, I'm just a wanker.'

By now the whole class was roaring with laughter, kids held their stomachs to try and control themselves, others stamped their feet. The teacher stood up to take control.

'OK, OK, you've had your fun, now calm down.'

Slowly, the noise level dropped and the debate continued, but it wasn't until Alem was on his way home that he found out why it was all so funny. Robert also informed him that he wasn't the first one to have had such tricks played on him. He then went on to explain some of the ruder English words to Alem.

Sometimes Alem would walk home with Buck; they lived in the same general direction. Buck was very different from Robert. He never brought his guitar to school but every time he had an opportunity he would be singing or writing songs. Most of the people who came into contact with him sensed that they were in the presence of a future superstar, albeit the kind that becomes famous for being doomy and gloomy. But Alem got on well with him because he was a thinker, not easily lead and always trying to work things out for himself. During one conversation Alem told him how much he loved school and when Buck asked him why, Alem said, 'Education, I want to be educated,' to which Buck replied, 'You can have an education and not be educated, and there is more to education than school.'

Alem missed seeing animals that weren't just pets, he missed the sounds of home, he missed the smell of its earth, the smell of its people and even the smell of cities. He missed playing outdoors; people seemed to be constantly moving from one concrete building to another. He was quick to notice that if he ran into a friend outside, they would inevitably ask where he was going. No one, it seemed, was ever just outside; the closest he could find to that was 'going for a walk'. Back home Alem had been used to making things, here it seemed that when kids wanted things they bought them, when they broke they replaced them. He missed playing creatively. Back home he once found a front bicycle wheel and decided to make a bike; he had to seek out and even manufacture parts. One day at Great Milford he was told by a boy that his parents had bought him a new bike because the front wheel had broken and his mum thought it was bad luck.

Alem's first major school holiday was Christmas. He knew that Christmas in London was going to be very different from Christmas back home, but he wasn't prepared for the huge amount of advertising that was targeted at him, and he was quietly amused at the way people celebrated Christmas without celebrating the birth of Christ. He listened to his fellow students constantly talking about what they wanted for Christmas but he was pleased to find out that the Fitzgeralds were very relaxed about the whole thing.

On Christmas Day Alem was woken up by Mr and Mrs Fitzgerald. Ruth had gone to a party the night before and was staying with a friend.

'Happy Christmas,' they said calmly, almost as if they were just saying good morning.

Mrs Fitzgerald walked over to the window and opened the curtains. 'Well, this is it, Alem, this is Christmas Day, east London style. Not much to it really. We're not that interested in Christmas, well, we don't rave about it anyway.'

Mr Fitzgerald took over. 'What we don't know is what kind of thing you would want for Christmas, so we decided to give you this,' he said, handing him a white envelope.

Alem sat up in bed and reached out to take the envelope. He opened it to find four crisp fifty pound notes in it.

'You can buy what you want with it, or you can save it for a rainy day.'

'What would I buy on a rainy day?' Alem asked.

'That's just a saying,' Mr Fitzgerald said. 'A rainy day just means when things are not going too well and you need a bit of help, so a rainy day could actually be a nice sunny day,' he said playfully.

'Don't confuse him,' Mrs Fitzgerald said. 'It's yours to do whatever you want with, Alem.'

On Christmas Day Alem read George Orwell's *Nineteen Eighty-Four*. On Boxing Day he started *Lord of the Flies* and finished it on 29th December. He rested on the thirtieth and on New Year's Eve, when it seemed like everyone else was counting down the hours and the minutes towards the new millennium, Alem walked to Barking Road and bought a brand-new thirty-speed bike.

CHAPTER 12

~ Court in Action ~

The bike was used regularly over the next few days as Alem began to expand his knowledge of the area. Even when riding his bike he would travel with a small notepad and pen to write down the names of streets and buildings that he thought were interesting. He quickly learned that many of the street names had a relevance to the history of the area or commemorated interesting people. Forest Gate used to be the gateway to Epping Forest, and not far from where he lived he discovered Wordsworth, Shakespeare, Shelley, Byron and Ruskin avenues and many other avenues named after famous writers. One day he rode his bike deep into the forest in the belief that he would spot some wild animals, but all he saw was a few squirrels, which seemed too nice to be called wild. He had heard that there were deer and foxes in the forest but he saw none of them.

The time of Alem's first major challenge was nearing and he was reminded of it when he received a visit from Mariam and Sheila on 6th January. In the living room Mariam began to explain to Alem and Mr and Mrs Fitzgerald what was going to happen. Sheila butted in from time to time when she felt that things were getting too technical and some emotional reassurance was necessary. The file that Mariam had on Alem looked as if it had doubled in size. She took a couple of sheets of paper from it and put it on the table.

'We really don't expect much to happen tomorrow, Alem. We certainly don't expect the adjudicator to make a decision.'

'Well, what will he do?' Alem asked.

'Oh, he'll just want to familiarise himself with the case. He may ask for some reports to be made and he may ask you a few questions.'

Alem looked worried. 'Will I have to make some kind of speech?'

'No,' Mariam replied, 'you may have to answer a few simple questions but most of the talking will be done by your barrister. His name is Nicholas Morgan and he's one of the best. He does a lot of these types of cases.'

'Don't worry,' Sheila said, smiling, 'you'll be all right.'

'So when will I see Nicholas Morgan?' Alem asked Mariam.

'You'll see him in the morning. But really, Alem, don't worry. He'll talk to you before you go into the court and he has already read a lot about you and your case.'

It took some time for Alem to get used to the idea that someone he had never met was going to represent him, but he soon realised that everyone knew what they were doing and he felt a bit better. However, he couldn't help thinking that he was about to face some kind of trial. He spent a couple of hours lying on his bed thinking of what was going to happen the next day, then he spent a couple of hours reading in order to stop thinking about what was going to happen the next day.

The next morning Alem was woken up by Mrs Fitzgerald, who entered his room carrying a black suit. 'Good morning, Alem. I got you this.' She held the suit up high by its hanger as if waiting for a response.

Alem wasn't sure how to respond. Was this something that he had earned, or was this something that he should put away for a rainy day? He rubbed his eyes. It took some time for the words to come out. These were his first words of the day, and they sounded as if they were left over from the day before. 'What – what is it for?'

'It's your suit,' Mrs Fitzgerald replied. 'You have to make a good impression in court and there's no better way to make a good impression than by wearing a smart suit.'

Alem had always avoided disagreement with the Fitzgeralds and he certainly didn't want to have one on a day like this, so he chose his words carefully. 'I thought that the barrister will be there to make a good impression for me, so he should be wearing a suit.'

'Very good,' Mrs Fitzgerald replied, acknowledging Alem's logic. 'But this is all about you, you'll be standing there right in front of the judge, he'll be looking straight at you. I know these things; a suit will make a good impression, take my word for it. I know how these people judge character.'

Alem rubbed his eyes again and paused for thought. 'If these judges are so intelligent, they should know that you cannot always judge by first impressions. They should know that a suit is just pieces of material sewn together and that you cannot judge a person's character by the pieces of material that they wear. And besides I thought the judge was going to look at the facts – why I'm here and can I stay, things like that. I didn't think he was going to judge my character.'

Mrs Fitzgerald looked down at Alem sitting up in the bed; the reasoning of this half-awake mind impressed her. 'You're right,' she said as she placed the suit across the bottom of the bed.

Alem looked at the suit. 'So I don't have to wear it then?'

She turned and began to leave the room. 'It's up to you.'

Half an hour later Alem looked in the wardrobe mirror and whispered to himself, 'I hate this suit.' The sleeves were too long, the legs were too long and the chest was too tight, but he felt that he had to wear it to please Mrs Fitzgerald.

'We have to leave soon,' Mr Fitzgerald shouted from downstairs. 'Get yourself together.'

Alem opened his door. 'Mr Fitzgerald, do I have to carry anything?'

'No, not really. You'll be back in no time,' he shouted back.

'Mr Fitzgerald, can I bring a book?'

'Of course you can,' Mr Fitzgerald replied. 'You won't have much time to read in court but you can read on the tube down if you like.'

Alem went to one of his piles of books and grabbed the one at the top of the pile; he then left the room and went downstairs without looking at what he had chosen. When he entered the living room, Mr and Mrs Fitzgerald were waiting for him. Ruth wandered about in her nightdress. It was the first time they had seen him in the suit. As they looked down, they all gasped as if horrified by some unsightly slime.

'Alem,' Mrs Fitzgerald said loudly, 'you can't do that – you can't wear trainers with that suit.'

Ruth shook her head. 'No, Alem, get real, it doesn't rock.'

He searched for more from Ruth. 'It doesn't rock?' he said. 'It doesn't rock what?'

'It don't go, it doesn't match,' she said.

Mr Fitzgerald circled around him as if inspecting a car. 'Everything's fine except the trainers.'

'Do you think I should change them?' Alem asked.

'I think you should,' Mr Fitzgerald replied. 'I think you should try wearing your shoes, the black ones we bought for you, they'll do nicely.'

After a short bus ride to East Ham Underground station they caught the tube and headed towards the court. Alem had not been outside the East End for a long time. Most journeys, no matter how small, would normally arouse some excitement in him but this morning he was very subdued. Fortunately they had all managed to find seats, but as the train moved closer to central London it began to fill up. By the time it had reached Mile End, the train was packed; there was standing room only, and very little of that. As the bodies filled the carriage, the temperature rose and Alem began to sweat in his heavy suit. The train rocked from side to side and forwards and backwards as it was braking and accelerating, and as it did so the only part of Alem that remained still was his feet, weighed down by his heavy shoes.

Alem wondered why the people on the train were

trying so hard not to be noticed. Some would just stare at the advertisement boards as if they were trying to see through them, some read newspapers or books as if they were being forced, some tried to go back to sleep, and others listened to music on their Walkman. But no one was making eye contact with him and no one smiled. These were the employed people, he thought, those that had left school and obtained jobs. They were not starving, they were not at war but they looked miserable. I wonder, Alem thought to himself, are they all going to court? There was nothing else for him to do so he opened his book.

The book turned out to be a collection of war poems by Wilfred Owen. Alem had not read much poetry but he soon tuned into what was in front of him. He quickly picked up on the big stories behind the sometimes short poems. He held the book tightly with both hands close to his chest, trying to minimise the amount of movement caused by the train. At times he would stop reading and look up to digest a verse, only to find that some of the faces had changed in the carriage but they were still pretty miserable.

Alem and the Fitzgeralds got off at Borough Underground station and walked to the court in Swan Street. It was a very old building, grey and lacking in colour. Alem felt that there was something menacing about the building, yet it had a timeless beauty about it. It looked as if giants had carved it by hand out of one solid piece of stone. They entered the building and were directed to the noticeboard, where Alem found his name along with many others.

'I found my name,' Alem told the others, who were still searching the many names.

'What does it say?' asked Mrs Fitzgerald.

Alem took a moment to read it through to himself, then he read it aloud. 'Case Number C651438, Appellant – Alem Kelo. Respondent – the Secretary of State. Ten o'clock, Court Number Nine.'

All four turned to look for signs giving directions. In this part of the building everybody looked as if they knew exactly where they were going, everybody looked so confident.

'Oh, I know where it is,' Mrs Fitzgerald exclaimed. 'It's upstairs, I know exactly where it is.'

'How do you know?' Alem asked as they all began to follow her.

'I've been here before with little Themba.'

'Who is little Themba?' Alem was trying to keep up with her as she strode up the stairs. Mr Fitzgerald lagged way behind.

'Themba was such a nice boy. He stayed with us a long time ago. We came here because they wanted to send him back.'

'Back to where?'

'Back to South Africa,' Mrs Fitzgerald said almost

as if Alem should have known. 'His mother and father were there but they didn't want Themba to grow up in a country that was officially racist. Nor did I.'

By now Alem was struggling not to burst into a run. 'Did he have to go back, Mrs Fitzgerald?'

Mrs Fitzgerald slowed down as they reached court number nine. A large figure 9 hung over the door. 'Now that's a long story. The court allowed him to stay, so he stayed for a while. Then, when Nelson Mandela was freed and things began to change, he went back and now he's a computer programmer. He still phones me sometimes.'

Outside courtroom number nine there were two other families. Both families looked anxious and both spoke languages that Alem couldn't recognise. There was just enough room left on the bench for Alem and the Fitzgeralds to sit. Alem looked down the corridor where he could see other numbered signs hanging outside courtrooms, with other families sitting in front of them. In this part of the building the people didn't look as though they knew where they were going, and these people certainly didn't look confident.

Small children walked up and down, some would try to communicate with others through touching and offering to share toys. Many of the adults smoked nervously. When Alem heard people speaking, he seemed to hear a different language every time. He sat and watched two small boys, one black African and one white European, colouring a book. Unable to communicate verbally, they smiled and made noises to each other as crayons magically left their colour on the pages. Suddenly, Alem heard a familiar voice.

'Hello, Alem – Mr and Mrs Fitzgerald.'

'Hello,' Alem replied.

It was Sheila; she was with a man in his late twenties with very short brown hair and a goatee beard. His grey suit, grey tie and white shirt all looked as if he had bought them that morning. He smiled.

'This is Nicholas Morgan,' Sheila said, 'I told you about him.'

'I hope she's told you some good things too,' he said, flashing his perfect teeth and his clean-cut smile.

Sheila had heard that one before. A little embarrassed, she began to introduce the family to Nicholas. 'This is Alem and this is Mr and Mrs Fitzgerald, his foster parents.'

Nicholas kept smiling. 'Pleased to meet you.'

He shook everyone's hands and then sat precariously on the bench next to Alem. As he spoke, he looked directly at Alem; his voice was clear, soft and sympathetic.

'Alem, I just need to chat a little about what's going to happen this morning. This case has arisen because the Secretary of State, in other words the government, has doubts about your reasons for being here.

What we have to do is convince the adjudicator that the reasons you put in the statement you made are legitimate. Now, today nothing much will happen. The adjudicator will ask you if you are Alem Kelo; the person that represents the state will stand up and say why he thinks you should go; and then I'll stand up and say why I think you should stay. The adjudicator should then ask us to go away and prepare our cases. It should be as simple as that. Do you have any questions?'

Alem looked around. 'Who are these people? Will they be in there too?' he asked with a slight nod of his head in the direction of the other people seated on the bench.

'No, these are other cases that will be heard after you. I think they're Polish Romany people, probably in a similar position to you,' Nicholas replied. He looked at his notes and pointed to something that he had spotted. 'There is an interpreter available if you want one but I've been told that you're happy without one. Is that right?'

'Yes, I think I'll be OK. Do you think my English is good enough?' he asked.

'I think you'll be fine,' Nicholas said as he reached out and touched Alem on his shoulder.

Nicholas stayed with them until a woman came from the courtroom and called out Alem's name.

Mrs Fitzgerald jumped up as if startled by a ghost.

'Oh, that's us!'

Nicholas led them into the courtroom. Mr and Mrs Fitzgerald went to the family seats, and Nicholas led Alem to his seat. Directly opposite was the adjudicator's seat. It was big, red and empty, and stood on a raised platform, which Alem immediately thought was to symbolise superiority. Mounted on the wall above the seat was a large gilded crest. It portrayed a large lion and unicorn facing each other; above them was a golden crown and below them were the Latin words '*Dieu et mon droit*'. In front of Alem to the left stood Nicholas, making last-minute notes, and to the right of him stood the representative of the Secretary of State. Underneath the adjudicator's platform sat the usher who had called Alem in, and to the left of her sat the clerk. The walls of the room were high, panelled halfway up in a rich, dark wood, but from there on up to the ceiling they were painted in cheap magnolia. Alem admired the panelling but noticed that the top half of the room had been neglected; the magnolia paint was flaking and cobwebs stretched from the corners and light fittings as if protected by a preservation order.

Suddenly, everyone stood up. Alem was taken by surprise; he was the only one left seated. He looked towards Nicholas, who signalled with his hand and mimed the words 'Stand up'. Alem stood up. The adjudicator walked in and sat in his seat and everyone sat down, except Alem. Nicholas signalled him down with his hand and mimed the words 'Sit down'. Alem sat down.

The hearing began as predicted. The state representative spoke first.

'The state believes that the appellant faces no personal threat if he were to be returned to his country. We are of the belief that if he were returned, he would live a relatively peaceful life.'

Next Nicholas stood up and said his piece. 'My client believes that he has much to fear if he were to return home at this time. He has in fact suffered persecution there in the past and the political circumstances in both Ethiopia and Eritrea have not changed since then.'

Alem watched the adjudicator as he read from some of the papers in front of him, and knew that he was reading about him. The adjudicator then turned to Alem, took off his spectacles and began to speak. 'What I am going to do is adjourn this hearing so that reports can be prepared. Do you understand?'

Alem was nervous, his reply was barely audible. 'Yes, I understand.'

The adjudicator continued. 'Until you come back before me, you will stay with your foster parents at 202 Meanly Road. Is that agreeable?'

'Yes,' Alem said more positively.

'Very well,' the adjudicator concluded. 'Do you

have anything to say?'

'Yes,' Alem replied.

There was a look of surprise on the face of Nicholas. He had no idea what Alem could possibly want to say; he just hoped that he wouldn't say anything that would jeopardise his case. The Fitzgeralds looked at each other, not knowing what was going to happen next. Alem wasn't working to the script.

Alem looked around the courtroom and said, 'I would like to wish you all a happy Christmas.'

A smile came to the faces of all in the courtroom and the clerk noted his remarks.

The adjudicator's tone changed, and he leaned forward and spoke to Alem as if he was genuinely trying to help him. 'It's difficult to tell whether you mean that in retrospect or are speaking of the Christmas to come. You see, we have just had Christmas.'

'I know,' Alem replied, 'people were very nice to me at Christmas, but today it is Christmas in Ethiopia and Eritrea and many other parts of the world, and I think that if Christmas makes us nicer to each other, we should celebrate as many Christmases as we can.'

There were smiles from all in the courtroom and quiet laughter from some. Mrs Fitzgerald smiled as tears rolled down her face.

The adjudicator laughed the loudest. 'Not only have I learned something new today, I have also been made wiser. I would like to thank you for imparting your knowledge to me and I would like to take this opportunity to wish you a happy Christmas.'

Alem smiled at the adjudicator. The adjudicator put on his spectacles and continued. 'This hearing will now be adjourned until 15 February on the condition that the appellant resides with his current foster parents. I hope by then that all the relevant reports can be prepared.'

The two representatives nodded. The adjudicator stood and the whole court stood. This time Alem followed the crowd. The adjudicator turned and left, whereupon the courtroom filled with talk as everyone began to leave.

The Fitzgeralds headed straight for Alem. Mr Fitzgerald shook his hand and said, 'You had us worried there for a moment.'

Mrs Fitzgerald hugged him, kissed him on his forehead and said, 'Alem, you were great! Happy Christmas!'

CHAPTER 13

~ Loved and Lost ~

The next day Alem was back in school. His English was improving by the day and he was tuning in well to the accent of east Londoners but he hadn't come to terms with the weather. Sometimes he would find himself shivering because of the bitter cold but he would not complain, he just told himself that one day he would get used to it.

Two days later Alem woke up as normal to the smell of breakfast being cooked. Thanks to the twin radiators the room was warm enough for him to push the quilt aside and have a good stretch. He jumped up, sat on the bed and reached down to pick up a book. The book that came to hand was *A History of the East End*, a book of large old black and white photographs with very little text. He flicked through the pages and would stop at certain photos that caught this eye. The first was a photo of Boleyn Castle. The picture had no people in it and the quality of the photo was poor. The words underneath claimed that Anne Boleyn had lived there, and Henry VIII courted her there in secret trysts. Then Alem turned to a picture taken in 1905 of 'The Ladies of the St John Ambulance Brigade'. They were all dressed in white frocks with black capes, and stared into the camera as if they were afraid of it. As Alem looked at them he wondered what they were thinking at the time, and who was St John? He flicked through pages of photos of old churches, famous people and industrial buildings, ending up on a picture of Beckton in the Blitz. A bomb had hit a row of houses in a street; they had been reduced to rubble. Alem looked deep into the photo and began to notice small details, which at first were not visible among the mass of bricks and piping. He saw shoes, a doll, a radio, a handbag and a couple of hats, one of which looked very much like the hats that were worn by the ladies of the St John Ambulance Brigade.

Alem put the book down and went to the window. 'Gosh!' he shouted loudly as he looked outside. 'That's something else!' Outside was foggy, frosty and cold.

'Mrs Fitzgerald!' he shouted. 'Have you seen outside?'

She shouted back, 'What's the matter?'

'Is there something wrong with the pond?' shouted Mr Fitzgerald.

'Yes,' Alem replied, 'the pond is disappearing, everything is so white.'

'That's nothing,' shouted Mr Fitzgerald. 'You should see it when it snows. It doesn't happen much nowadays, but that's when it's really white.'

At the breakfast table Mr Fitzgerald explained that England was like that. 'You could get four seasons in a day sometimes,' he said trying to make it sound like an original observation. He went on to give a lecture on how unlucky the kids were now, and how when he was young snow would be around for weeks and they would make sleighs and snowmen. 'But not now,' he said, 'it's that global-warming thing, it never really freezes for long and if you want a snowman nowadays you can go and buy a blow-up one in the shop.'

The frost fascinated Alem, but he hadn't prepared himself for walking to school in it. He opened the front door and the cold hit him, and even though he was warmly dressed, his puffer jacket couldn't stop him from feeling it. He stepped carefully down the short path and turned to wave goodbye.

That morning the whole atmosphere of the streets had changed, he thought. Cars, people, even the air felt as if it was moving more slowly. The cats and dogs looked streetwise and tough, and the birds sang louder. He looked up at two birds singing to each other in a tree on the street and wondered how the small fragile creatures could survive in such conditions. The birds seemed quite happy and didn't sound as if they were complaining.

As the day progressed the temperature rose and by dinnertime the ice had completely disappeared. But the cold stayed around to remind Alem that he was far away from home.

That afternoon when Alem came home from school he was told that Mariam was on her way to see him. By the time he had changed his clothes she had arrived. This time she was looking worried and Alem wasted no time with pleasantries.

'What is the matter?' he asked, looking Mariam directly in her eyes.

Mariam couldn't hide her anxiety. She took a letter from the folder she was holding and handed it to Alem. He went straight up to his room, sat on his bed and opened the letter.

My dearest son,

I am afraid that I have to tell you some very bad news. Remember I told you in my last letter that darkness is upon the land? Well, my son, please prepare yourself for what I have to say. This is very bad news, because darkness is now upon our family. After searching for many weeks I have just learned that your mother is no longer with us. She was killed by some very evil people and left near the border.

Please, son, I want you to be strong, now I need you to be strong more than ever, and your mother would want you to be strong. It is very difficult for me here now, I don't feel

155

that I have anything here any more, so in the next few days I will be leaving here and joining you. At this time I think that it is important that we must be together so I am coming. I will find you through the Refugee Council and we will be together again.

I long to see you and I promise you I will be with you soon, so be strong, be as strong as your mother, and we will make it through the darkness.

Your loving father

Downstairs, Mariam explained to Mr and Mrs Fitzgerald that, like the last one, the letter had arrived at the Refugee Council, this time accompanied by another letter addressed to the council itself, explaining the circumstances behind Alem's arrival in Britain and informing them of the death of Alem's mother.

When he heard about the death, Mr Fitzgerald fell into his armchair and whispered, 'I don't believe it. The poor boy!'

Mrs Fitzgerald headed for the door to go upstairs. 'I must go and talk to him. He can't be left up there all by himself,' she said, almost pushing Mariam over as she passed her.

'No, no,' Mariam said softly, 'take it easy. Just give him a little time to himself. It's a lot for him to take in.'

Against her instincts, Mrs Fitzgerald stayed downstairs. She offered Mariam a cup of tea, Mariam accepted, and as the three of them sat drinking, Ruth came home. Ruth was given the bad news and was stunned into silence.

After an hour of very few words, Mariam decided that it was time to leave. She wrote down the number of her mobile phone and gave it to Mrs Fitzgerald. 'Do ring me any time if you need any help, any time, day or night.'

In the hallway she told Mr and Mrs Fitzgerald that they should keep an eye on Alem and try to speak to him soon. 'I would just like to say something to him before I leave.'

She followed Mrs Fitzgerald up to Alem's room, where she spoke to him through the closed door. 'Alem, I must go now, but I'm going to ring you tomorrow, and I've left my mobile number with Mr Fitzgerald, so if you need me for any reason at all, at any time, please ring me, OK?'

'Yes,' came the reply from the other side of the door, but Alem said nothing else and Mariam left.

Not long afterwards Alem made his way slowly downstairs. Mr and Mrs Fitzgerald were moving between the kitchen and the dining room, preparing the evening meal, and Ruth sat in the living room reading a magazine. When Mrs Fitzgerald saw Alem in the dining room, she quickly put down the casserole dish she was carrying and went to him. She wrapped her arms around him and kissed his forehead. 'You poor boy, it must be so hard for you! Don't worry, son, we'll look after you.'

Ruth came into the dining room and went straight to Alem. 'Are you all right?' she asked.

'I'm OK,' Alem replied.

At the meal everyone was cautious. All the members of the family were concerned with Alem's state of mind. Although he was quiet and looked very much in control, none of them knew how much Alem would want to talk about things. Alem was eating very little, very slowly.

'Eat as much as you can, dear,' said Mrs Fitzgerald gently.

'Yes, Mrs Fitzgerald,' Alem replied.

For a long time the only sound coming from the room was that of the cutlery scraping the porcelain.

'Try and eat some more,' Mrs Fitzgerald said. 'Eating may not seem that important to you now, and it may not be the best food in the world, but I reckon there's a few of those vitamin and mineral things in there.'

'And we all need some of those,' Mr Fitzgerald added.

Then it was back to the silence. Another couple of minutes passed and Alem put down his knife and fork as he stared into his food.

Ruth was the first to notice. 'What's the matter?' she asked.

Suddenly, Alem burst into tears and began crying loudly. He stamped his feet up and down and began hitting the sides of his clenched fists against his thighs, causing glasses of water to topple on the table. He cried louder, then he put his hands over his ears and shook his head as if he was trying to keep out an evil sound. His sobbing was becoming harder to control; he tried to shout some words in Amharic but that just made him lose control even more. He quickly stood up. The table shook as his thighs hit it, his chair fell to the floor behind him and he ran upstairs.

They listened to him from downstairs for a while as he cried. He gasped for breath as the crying sapped the energy from him, then they could hear him talking loudly to himself in Amharic, ranting as if he had lost his mind. They couldn't understand what he was saying but somehow it sounded as if he was pleading with someone or begging for something. Slowly, he began to quieten down. They listened as he drew in big, deep breaths; they could hear him trying his best to pull himself together.

The house fell silent and for a while the Fitzgeralds moved around as quietly as they could, trying not to disturb him. They lowered their voices as they spoke and made sure not to slam any doors. In the dining room they held an impromptu family meeting to decide what to do next.

It was decided that Mrs Fitzgerald should go up,

but as she was leaving the room, Ruth called to her.

'Mum, let me go.'

Mrs Fitzgerald thought this was very uncharacteristic of Ruth. 'So why do you want to go? The last thing we want to do is upset him any more.'

But Ruth sounded as if she meant business. 'Just let me go, Mum, I know what I'm doing.'

Ruth knocked on the door as lightly as she could. There was no response. She knocked a little louder. Still no response. Then she knocked even louder but there was still no response.

She turned the door handle and began to speak as she opened the door. 'Alem, Alem, are you all right?'

She popped her head round the door to find Alem fast asleep on the bed. He was fully dressed and curled up on the bed in the foetal position. Ruth closed the door and went back downstairs.

About an hour later the phone rang. Mrs Fitzgerald quickly picked it up so that it wouldn't wake Alem. It was Sheila. She explained to Mrs Fitzgerald that she had heard the news and wanted to offer her help. She also asked that Alem should not be sent to school the next day because she needed to see him, as did Nicholas the barrister. They spoke about the way Alem had reacted to the news, but Mrs Fitzgerald insisted that things were now under control and that if she needed her help or that of the Social Services, she would let them know.

As the call was ending, Ruth heard movement in Alem's room. She quickly went to the bottom of the stairs to listen, and when she was sure she went up and quietly knocked on his door.

'Come in,' Alem said.

She entered the room where Alem was sitting on his bed, re-stacking the books which he had knocked over.

'Alem, are you all right?' she asked sympathetically.

'I'm OK,' said Alem, still in his monotone mode.

Ruth stood next to the bed. 'There's no way I can feel exactly what you're feeling now but I just wanna tell you that I'm here for you, right? Whatever you want, right, I'm here.'

Alem just nodded his head. Ruth continued. 'It's bad, yeah, but you gotta be strong, right, and if we stick together we'll be strong, innit?'

Alem nodded his head again. Ruth pressed on. 'There's a load of bullshit happening out there, you know. There's wars, famines, you got all those politicians talking rubbish, you got all those people believing the rubbish, and when it comes down to your mates, you just don't know who to trust. Well, I'm letting you know, Alem, you can trust me. Whatever's going down, right, you can trust me. I'm like your sister, right?'

The thought lines on Alem's forehead deepened as he brought his eyebrows together. He couldn't work it out. Why was she being so nice to him now? Was she for real, and could he trust her?

'I know what you're thinking,' she said. 'Let me explain, Alem. We've had nine foster children here. The one before the last one used to go into my room and steal all my things, and the last one attacked me in the middle of the night. Some are good and some are bad, but how do I know who's who? One accused me of being a witch, and I fell in love with another. They just come and go and I have to be nice to all of them. I have nothing against *you*, Alem; I'm just a bit too suspicious, I suppose. And my parents, they've forgotten about me. I've got to be Little Miss Perfect now that I've left school and stand on me own two feet while they help the poor and needy. Well, I'm needy too. That's all, Alem. I ain't got nothing against you. It's my parents. They're good people, but they're just not good to me.'

She stopped for a moment and sat next to him on the bed before continuing. 'That's what it's about, it's like that. But I know that you're cool, everyone says you're no problem, and I know you're no problem so let's just chill. Why create bad vibes? Look, I'm sorry. Now remember this, no bad vibes, I'm like your sister, right?'

Alem turned his head slowly to look at her.

'Right?' she repeated, trying to get some response from him.

Alem suddenly lunged towards her with his arms outstretched. He put his arms around her, placing his head on her shoulder, and cried. This time he cried softly, squeezing her tightly. He had been hugged, but he had not hugged anyone since leaving Africa. Ruth could feel that he desperately needed to hold someone. She was taken by surprise but sat still and didn't move at all, and Alem didn't want her to move. He felt cold, and the heat from her body comforted him. His grip was tight and although his strength slightly restricted Ruth's ability to breathe, she relaxed and as slowly as she could she put her arms gently around him. She could feel his tears penetrating her clothes as they dropped on to her shoulder, but she could also feel Alem hugging the family he was missing.

CHAPTER 14

~ Life After Death ~

Sheila and Nicholas arrived at the house at half past ten the next morning. Ruth had phoned in to work and told the manager that there had been a death in her family, so all three of the Fitzgeralds were present. Mrs Fitzgerald had tea prepared; Mr Fitzgerald sat quietly in his chair and Ruth sat reading a music magazine, trying hard not to make it obvious that she was keeping an eye on Alem. Alem was quiet too; he had not managed to sleep much, his eyes were bloodshot and his skin had lost its shine.

As Sheila and Nicholas entered the living room, Sheila went straight to Alem and asked if she could speak to him privately in his room. Alem said yes and they made their way upstairs leaving the others drinking tea.

They both stood just inside the door as Sheila began speaking. 'I'm so sorry to hear about your mother,' she said softly. 'It really is terrible and you must be really feeling it. Is there anything you would like me to do for you, anything at all?'

Alem looked down and shook his head.

'Are you sure?' she added.

Still looking down, he nodded his head again.

'Well, look, Alem, all you have to do is ask and we'll do all we can. You know you can always talk to me if there's anything you need, and if you feel that you want to talk to anyone else, you know, a counsellor, then we can arrange that for you.'

'What's a counsellor?' Alem asked inquisitively.

'That's someone to talk to. Sometimes it helps if there is someone not connected with your family or your life who can listen to you and talk with you. It may not sound like much but it really can help when you have a lot of things on your mind. Would you like me to set up a meeting with one for you?' she asked in a way that suggested that he should say yes.

'No,' Alem replied, 'at the moment I don't feel like I want to talk to anyone.'

'Well, if you need me or anyone else to talk to, just say so. But Alem, just for a short time we will need you to talk to us. You see, Nicholas is here because he really needs to speak to you. You don't have to if you don't want to but it would help. He will have to ask you some questions about your case and possibly about your mother. Honestly, it would be very helpful.'

'That's OK.'

'It is important,' she continued, 'but if it's getting too much for you, just tell him to stop.'

Back in the living room Nicholas began to speak as soon as Alem sat down. 'Alem, I'm sorry to hear about what happened to your mother, you must be devastated. I may just be a man in a suit but I do understand what it's like to lose a loved one. My condolences, mate.'

Alem could see that for all Nicholas's smooth talk and his confident attitude, he did seem sincere. Nicholas always sounded as if he knew exactly what he was going to say before he said it, but this time Alem felt that he was searching for words. As Nicholas continued, he flipped back to his old self, conscious but businesslike.

'Alem, we have a problem. The opposition know that your father wrote to you in November and we have reason to believe that they want to drag the case out and possibly try to locate your father. Of course we know that the last letter you received from your father is a very painful one, but we would like to use it in court next month to strengthen your case. We can only do this with your permission.'

Alem thought for a while and all the eyes in the room were upon him. He turned to Sheila. 'Sheila, you are my social worker, yes?'

'Yes,' Sheila replied.

'You are concerned about my welfare, yes?'

'Yes,' said Sheila, not sure where this line of questioning was going.

'Well, don't you think that I should now go back and be with my father? Don't you think that now it is important that what is left of my family should be together?'

This was Alem being logical again. Everyone in the room looked at each other, knowing that there was some truth in what he was saying.

'Look, Alem, we cannot tell you to stay or to go,' Sheila responded. 'Quite frankly, if you were to seek political asylum because I told you to, I'd be in trouble. We are all just here for you. It's not our job to advise you on whether you should stay or not, but if you do want to stay, we will support you. All I can say to you is look at the facts. You've tried to live on both sides of the border and both communities have persecuted you. You've just lost your mother, and your father is in fear of his life. You would have no one to meet you when you arrive in Ethiopia or Eritrea and now you don't even have the address of a single relative there. You could be arriving there as your father is arriving here. Think about it. Why would you want to put your life in danger? We can't tell you what to do, Alem, but I think your father wants you to be as safe as possible. That's all I can say, it's up to you.'

Alem's response was immediate. 'Yes, but I'm not wanted here. Look, I have to go to court to stay here. In the papers they call us names. This country may be good for some things but if this country was so good,

why do I have to go to court to get some of this good-
ness? Why do they not believe me?'

Ruth and her parents sat with their heads bowed as
if they were being told off. Sheila sat back in her
chair. 'You have a point, Alem, but you must try to
understand the court system here, and let me assure
you that there are many people here who do welcome
you, you know that.'

At this point Nicholas entered the conversation. 'If
you like, you can think about it for a time. We don't
have to make a decision now, but the sooner we know
what evidence we have at our disposal, the more
effectively we can plan our strategy.'

'I will think about it now,' Alem said, and the room
fell silent again as everyone tried to listen to Alem
thinking.

All except for Mrs Fitzgerald. 'Fresh tea, anyone?'
she asked, smiling as if she had just come up with a
great idea. Everyone just shook their heads and continued to wait for Alem.

'OK,' Alem said, 'we must continue. You can use
the letter.'

Alem went up to his room and returned with the
letter and Ruth volunteered to go and get it photocopied at the newsagent's. When she returned, she
gave the original back to Alem and then gave a copy
each to Sheila and Nicholas, who began to read it
straightaway.

Nicholas read it quickly, put it into his case, then stood up. 'Alem, this is going to be hard for you but as Sheila said, we're all here to help. Hopefully this letter will make things a lot easier for us. I must go now, but there is still a month to go before the hearing so you get on with your life, leave this to us.'

Sheila was the next to stand up. 'See you soon, Alem.'

In the hallway the Fitzgeralds thanked Sheila and Nicholas before returning to the living room for a family meeting. Ruth took control; she suggested that Alem should have a couple of days off school and it was agreed. Her mother said she would phone the school and explain the situation, and Alem was told once more to get on with his life and to leave all the worrying to the barrister and the Social Services.

For the next couple of days Alem stayed at home. He spent much of the time reading or on his computer, and he even spent a little time in the garden with Mr Fitzgerald, feeding the fish and watching them swim round in circles. Ruth continued to go to work as normal but when she was home she now communicated with Alem a lot more. The night before he went back to school, she went for a long walk with him around the streets of Manor Park. After the walk, as Alem was sitting quietly in his room looking at the family photo, Ruth knocked on the door. Alem invited her in and she sat at his computer desk.

'Do you know how to use this thing?' she said, looking at the various pieces of hardware.

'I can do a few things, games, CD-ROMs, that's about all really.'

'Do you mind if I use it?' she asked.

'No, not at all. Do you want me to go for a while?'

'No,' said Ruth, 'but can I have a look at your photo?'

Alem handed her the photo. 'How old were you when this was taken?' she asked, looking at the happiness on the faces.

'Twelve,' Alem replied.

'Do you have any more photos?'

'No, just that one, and that one is wearing out because it has been in my bag, in my pockets, under my pillow, and I keep holding it.'

'Come here and watch me,' Ruth said, smiling.

Alem stood over her as she booted up the computer and began to work. Her speed and expertise astounded him. Within twenty minutes she had scanned in the photo and made it into his desktop image.

'There you go,' she said, leaning back to admire her handiwork. 'From now on every time you boot up your computer, that's what you'll get.'

Alem thought it was wonderful. The photo had grown to about six times its original size. He stood, jaw

170

hanging and mouth open, in awe of the technology.

'You don't like it? I can wipe it off,' she said, not sure of how he was taking it.

'No,' Alem said, 'I like it very much! It's very good, thank you, thank you very much.'

When Alem returned to school, nothing had changed. He thought that nobody had missed him, until school was over and he was speaking to Robert on the way home.

'So you been having some time out then?' Robert asked as he lit his cigarette.

'I had to,' Alem replied.

' What, you had to have a holiday?'

'I haven't been on holiday,' said Alem.

'What, you been sick or something?'

'No,' Alem said, not giving anything away.

Alem was a little more serious than his normal self but Robert thought this was about keeping a secret more than anything else.

He began to tease Alem. 'So you haven't been on holiday, you haven't been sick. I get it, you're in love!' His shoulder barged Alem, causing him to walk into someone's garden hedge.

Alem kept cool. 'I have love in my heart but I'm not in love.'

Robert continued to tease Alem even more, smiling broadly as he spoke. 'Hey, guy, stop all that wise talk.

Never mind all that "love in my heart" stuff, who you snogging, man, and why you so serious? It can't be that bad.'

Alem stopped. Robert turned to face him. 'Go on then, tell us, who it is?'

Alem looked him in the face, took in a deep breath and said, 'My mother has died.'

'What?' Robert replied, genuinely confused. 'You shouldn't joke about stuff like that, you know.'

Alem kept eye contact with him. 'I am not joking. My mother was killed and left on the border of Ethiopia and Eritrea.'

'Ethiopia!' Robert said aghast. 'Eritrea! What the hell she doing there?'

'That is where she lived.'

Robert was now really confused. He looked into Alem's eyes, then looked skywards and then back to Alem. 'I thought you lived on Meanly Road.'

'I do,' Alem replied, 'but with foster parents. I told you that I come from Ethiopia.'

'Yes,' Robert answered.

'And I told you that I come from Eritrea.'

'Yes,' said Robert. 'I couldn't work that one out, but I don't know the difference, do I? I thought it was the same place.'

'Well,' Alem said as they continued to walk, 'I am half Ethiopian and half Eritrean. Ethiopia and Eritrea are fighting each other and they are both fighting me,

172

that's why I had to come here as a refugee.'

'And where is your father?' Robert asked.

'I'm not sure but he did say he was going to try and come to England.'

Without realising it, Robert had walked to Alem's house. Alem asked Robert to wait outside the house. He went inside to ask Mrs Fitzgerald if Robert could come in.

'Of course,' she said. 'If he's your friend, he's my friend.'

Alem told Robert that his foster parents were called Mr and Mrs Fitzgerald. Inside, Alem discovered that Robert could display quite good manners when necessary.

'Hello, Mrs Fitzgerald,' he said, carefully wiping his feet on the doormat, 'pleased to meet you.'

'Hello, young Robert,' she replied. 'Would you like a cup of tea?'

'Yes, please.'

She turned to Alem. 'Drink?'

'Could I have a cola please? And can I take Robert into the garden?' Alem asked.

'Of course you can.'

In the back garden the two found Mr Fitzgerald replacing broken paving stones around the fishpond.

'Hello, Mr Fitzgerald,' Alem said, 'this is Robert.'

'Hello, Robert,' said Mr Fitzgerald. 'Do you like fish?'

'They're all right,' said Robert cautiously.

'Look,' said Alem, 'look at these ones! And there's a really big one in there that likes to stay near the bottom, you have to really look good to see him.'

'What kind of fish are they?'

'Koi,' said Alem, 'and the more water they have, the longer they live.'

'That's right,' said Mr Fitzgerald. He pointed deep into the pond. 'That's the oldest one there.'

Robert looked into the deep and spotted the large golden fish. 'How old is he?'

'Nine,' replied Mr Fitzgerald very proudly as if it was one of his children, 'and he's still got plenty of life in him yet.'

'Tea's ready,' shouted Mrs Fitzgerald at the back door.

In the dining room Robert drank his tea in a way that Alem had never seen before. He put five teaspoons of sugar in his tea, blew on it for three minutes and then drank it in one go. Alem looked on in amazement as he sipped his cola.

Mrs Fitzgerald popped her head in from the kitchen. 'Alem, why don't you take Robert to your room? It's a bit of a mess – but it's your mess.'

Upstairs in Alem's room Robert was surprised at how tidy it was. 'This isn't untidy! You wanna see my room, guy. What's untidy about this?' he asked, doing a full turn.

'That's untidy,' Alem said, pointing to the books on the floor, 'and so is that,' he said, pointing to the CD-ROMs scattered around the computer.

'You're crazy, guy,' Robert said, shaking his head. 'Why do you want to read so much after school?'

'Because I need to learn. I have to catch up with everyone else, and I like reading. Watch this,' Alem added, turning on the computer. They waited for a while until the computer was fully booted up and the photo appeared.

'That is my mother and father,' Alem said with sadness in his voice.

'Wow, your parents look cool! They look like a king and a queen. Shame about your mum, guy. How did you get the picture on there anyway?' Robert asked, changing the subject quickly.

Alem took the photograph from the bedside drawer and handed it to Robert. 'Ruth, that's Mr and Mrs Fitzgerald's daughter, she took this photograph, scanned it in, saved it in a file, then she just allocated it to be my desktop picture.'

'Wow, that's nutty, guy.' Robert looked at it for a moment. 'Don't you have no brothers or sisters?'

'No,' said Alem, 'just me.'

Robert looked into the drawer from which Alem had taken the photo and could see newspaper clippings. 'What are you collecting them for?'

'Because they are about refugees and I have to read

about why people don't like refugees.'

'Yes,' Robert said, 'but listen, guy. I done history in school and this country is full of refugees, especially here in Newham. Seriously, we're all refugees here. You wanna know my real name? My real name ain't Robert Fern, you know, it's Roberto Fernandez. Spanish name, guy. I came from Chile.'

Robert was surprised at how much Alem was surprised. 'You came here from Chile?' Alem asked wide-eyed.

'No, I was born here, but my mother and father did. In Chile there was this big football stadium and the man who used to run the country, his name was Pinochet, he took people there that didn't agree with him and he killed them, right in the national football stadium. And my auntie was killed there. She used to work for a newspaper or a magazine or something like that. Anyway, she was killed, my uncle just disappeared, so my mum and dad came here.'

Alem was shocked by what he was hearing. 'So are your parents all right now?'

'Yes,' Robert replied.

'But why did you change your name?' Alem asked.

'I don't know,' Robert replied, 'it wasn't my idea. My dad said our roots are still Chilean but we would fit in better if we changed our names a little. My mum's name is Cecile, she calls herself Cilla. My dad's name is Ricardo, and he calls himself Richard.'

176

Alem looked horrified but Robert continued. 'Don't be so shocked, guy. I know a Birinder called Bernie, an Anula called Ann, a Rajinder called Ray, and I know this other girl, right, she's beautiful, her name's Nosayarba but she calls herself Ni. Check it out, guy, people do it all the time.'

'So who went to war against Chile?' Alem asked.

'It's a bit like where you come from, Chile just went to war with itself.'

'Do you want to go back to Chile some day?'

'Go back!' Robert said loudly. 'I don't really feel like I even come from there. My mum and dad haven't been there for years and they keep going on about returning one day. But me, how can I return to a place that I've never been to? Just because I eat a bit of Chilean food and listen to a bit of Chilean music, that don't make me Chilean. Well, I don't think so anyway. I'd better go home now.'

They went downstairs to the kitchen, where Robert said goodbye to Mr Fitzgerald in the garden and Mrs Fitzgerald who was cooking. 'Are you sure you won't stay for a bite to eat, Robert?'

'No, thank you,' Robert replied.

'Another cup of tea?'

'No, thank you, Mrs Fitzgerald. I have to be home. Is it all right if me and Alem go out together tomorrow after school, Mrs Fitzgerald? It is Friday.'

Alem looked surprised. He didn't expect Robert to

177

ask such a question.

Mrs Fitzgerald turned to face Robert. 'Where are you going then?'

'I don't know yet, anywhere, just out. We won't go far, maybe go visit another friend or something like that.'

'That's OK,' she replied, 'so long as you're back by nine o'clock and you don't get into trouble.' She looked towards Alem. 'It would do you good to get out with your friends.'

At the door Alem expressed his surprise. 'Where are we going tomorrow?'

'I don't know but don't worry, you heard what Mrs Fitzgerald said, it'll do you good. See you tomorrow,' Robert said, walking to the gate.

'OK, Roberto,' Alem said, surprising Robert.

He turned and took a couple of steps back towards Alem. 'Just Robert, guy. Roberto confuses me a bit. It's all right. I'm not ashamed of it or anything, but it just reminds me of someone my parents want me to be.'

CHAPTER 15

~ The Africans ~

After school the next day Alem and Robert went to their respective homes to eat and change their clothes. At five-thirty Robert was knocking at Alem's front door.

'Let's go,' he said impatiently, rubbing his hands together while lightly jogging on the spot, trying to keep warm.

Alem had been eagerly waiting. He stepped out and shouted goodbye before closing the door. As they reached the street pavement, Alem asked where they were going.

'I don't know,' Robert said, 'we're just going out, innit, hanging out.'

'But Robert, don't you think it's a bit cold to just hang out? If we hang out for long enough we will freeze.'

'I know.' Robert's eyes lit up. 'Let's go and listen to some music.'

'What kind of music?' Alem asked.

'Some rock, grungy stuff, Buck's band, yeah. Let's listen to Buck's band, they're rehearsing tonight.'

Alem was hesitant. 'OK but where do they rehearse?'

'Not far. Katherine Road, in the basement of a shop.'

Twenty minutes later they were pressing the doorbell but there was no response. They could hear the bell, but because of the music the band couldn't hear it. Robert waited for a while and when a song ended he quickly rang the bell again, pressing as hard as he could until the door was opened by Buck. He was dressed in flared jeans, a T-shirt with a large tongue on it and a hooded parka.

'All right?' Robert said. 'We've come to hear you do some tunes.'

Buck turned and headed back down to the cellar. 'No sweat, but I'm warning you, geezer, it's the tunes that are doing us.'

The cellar was damp with whitewashed walls. Various bands who had rehearsed there had left their graffiti tags on the walls, and the carpet was more wet than damp and reeked of stale beer. Buck wrapped himself in his guitar and joined the rest of the band. Alem and Robert sat on the upturned beer crates that represented audience seating.

Buck had his microphone adjusted to the height of his forehead so he had to stretch his neck and turn his face skyward to sing into it. The other guitarist, the bass player and the drummer looked like clones of

Buck, wearing flared jeans, or new jeans that had been ripped at the knees, and parkas or combat-type jackets. The keyboard player was different, she was a girl. She wore clean straight jeans with no holes, a woollen jumper, a warm full-length coat and small glasses that made her look like a young, sensible intellectual.

'They're called Pithead,' Robert said, smiling.

'Who?'

'All of them,' Robert said as the band checked their tuning. 'The band's name is Pithead, apparently it's got something to do with being working class.'

'Ready?' said Buck. Band members nodded or made various noises. 'OK – one – two – three – four,' and they started the song.

As they played, Alem watched in amazement as Buck moaned over the gloomy, downbeat music. Alem couldn't understand the words but he thought Buck's voice matched the music well, he seemed to cry over music that cried. They played three songs one after the other and then stopped for a break. Buck introduced the rest of the band to Alem, but they quickly left to buy something to eat and drink.

Buck sat on a beer crate. 'What do you think of the noise, Alem?'

Alem nodded his head towards the instruments as if there was still music coming from there. 'What kind of music is that?'

'It's called, indie music.'

'What, you mean Indian music?'

'No,' said Buck, 'indie music, man, independent music. It's the sound of the street, it's our music, the sound of the youth. This music ain't controlled by men in suits or capitalist fat cats. This music helps free up the minds because the music is free, you know what I mean, independent.'

'I understand,' said Alem.

'Do you?' said Robert sarcastically. 'I don't.'

'And what do you want to do next?' Alem asked.

'Well, we're trying to sign a record deal with a good record label.'

Alem responded quickly. 'But signing a record deal with a record label means you won't be independent.'

Robert began to laugh. Alem was seriously trying to make sense of what Buck was saying, and Buck was a little lost for words.

'Well, we need money, so if we get the money from the record company, we can afford to be independent and do our own thing.'

'But it won't be your own thing,' Alem insisted, 'it will be owned by the company.'

'Look, man,' Buck said. 'At the end of the day it don't matter, it's all in the mind. Check it out, all this stuff is not happening, it ain't real. Death is real, geezer, nothing is the truth.'

Alem's expression was blank. He looked towards Robert, who raised his eyebrows and looked around the room. Robert then looked at Buck and said, 'Do you know any jokes?'

'Are you trying to be funny?' Buck retorted, sounding deadly serious.

'No, I'm serious, guy. You're always on a downer, you're always being miserable, guy, and you got the money in the bank – your dad's loaded. Why don't you make some dance music instead of making everyone depressed?'

Buck stood up. 'The masses are brainwashed, people need to hear the truth.'

Robert stood up too. 'Yeah, guy, but can't you put the truth on a nice beat?'

'Listen, geezer,' Buck said, smiling for the first time. 'You can't make the truth funny and anyway, look at the state of you! You depress me.'

'Yeah,' Robert replied, laughing, 'and I hope you remember me when you make lots of money from depression.'

The rest of the band could be heard making their way back down the cellar stairs.

'We better go,' Robert said, 'we got lots to do.'

'What we got to do?' Alem asked, unsure what Robert had in mind.

'Lots,' he replied.

Alem stood up. 'OK, see you soon,' he said to Buck.

They bid the rest of the band goodbye and were

soon walking down Katherine Road with nowhere to go.

'So, what are we going to do now?' Alem asked.

'I don't know,' Robert said as if he was surprised by the question.

'But you said we got lots to do.'

'I just wanted to get out of that smelly cellar, it stinks. I know, let's go to Stratford Centre,' Robert replied.

'What is there?'

'Nothing, it's just a shopping centre where we can hang out until we get moved on by the security or the police.'

'So you just go there and wait around until you get told to move?'

'That's right,' Robert said excitedly, 'then we go away and come back later.'

'That's it?' Alem said. 'You get moved, then you return?'

'Yeah, it's fun.'

Alem shook his head. 'I don't think so, it doesn't sound like fun to me.'

'I got an idea,' Robert shouted. 'Yeah, I know! Let's go to Asher's house – you'll like him, he's Ethiopian or Eritrean or something like that.'

Alem became very thoughtful and didn't respond straightaway. Then he asked, 'What do you mean "something like that", don't you know where he's

184

from? Are you sure he's even from Africa?'

'Yeah, I'm sure he's from Ethiopia, he keeps going on about it. Anyway, why do you look so worried?' he asked, noticing Alem's change of mood.

'Because you don't know where he really comes from and I told you about my situation. He could be Ethiopian and not like me because I'm Eritrean, or he could be Eritrean and not like me because I'm Ethiopian.'

Robert laughed. 'Are you joking – Asher? Asher couldn't hate anyone if he tried; all he talks about is peace and love. He goes on about world peace and vegetarianism, he wouldn't even know how to make a fist. And anyway, just because Eritreans and Ethiopians are fighting in Africa, that don't mean the kids are fighting here.'

Alem agreed to go and see Asher but he was still a little concerned. Asher lived about ten minutes away from the cellar, in Halley Road. As they approached the house, Alem began to ask questions, partly out of genuine curiosity and partly to cover up his nervousness. 'So how old is he?'

'Seventeen, he's at college.'

'What does he study?'

'Music technology and business studies.'

'How do you know him?'

'He used to go to our school but he's left now.'

Robert rang the bell of the first-floor flat. The door was opened very quickly by a brown-skinned boy with a broad nose and the beginnings of a moustache. He had thick dreadlocks that hung down to just below his chest. He was wearing large baggy jeans, the baggiest Alem had ever seen, and a deep-blue fleece.

'What's up?' said Asher with a broad smile. He looked at Alem. 'How's it going, brother?'

'OK,' Alem replied almost shyly.

'Come in,' Asher said, gesturing to them with his hands.

The living room was painted red, yellow and green and all the walls were empty except one which had a large picture of Haile Selassie, the last emperor of Ethiopia. Furniture in the room was kept to a minimum. One three-seater settee, a coffee table, a small portable television in one corner and a bookshelf in the other. A large West African drum doubled up as a stand for a Nubian head carving, and large beanbags on the floor made for additional seating.

Alem was captivated by Asher's demeanour. Around his neck from a gold chain hung a piece of wood, carved in the shape of Africa. Alem took to him immediately but he was sure that he wasn't from Ethiopia or Eritrea; in fact, as far as Alem could see, he didn't even look as if was from East Africa.

Alem and Robert sat on the settee; Asher sat on a

beanbag. 'What's happening?' he said, still smiling.

'Nothing,' Robert replied. 'I wanted you to meet Alem, he goes to Great Milford.'

'Cool, man,' Asher said, nodding his head and looking at Alem. 'So how long you been going there?'

'About three months now,' Alem replied.

'Do you like it?'

'It's OK,' Alem said, 'but I don't know how good it is compared to others because it's the first school that I have been to in England.'

'Yeah, I get what you're saying – where do you come from?'

'I come from Africa – Ethiopia, Eritrea – that's where I come from.'

Asher's eyes lit up. 'Yes, Rasta, I knew it! Ethiopia, the motherland, the land where the gods love to be! As soon as I saw you I said, There's a God son, a true child of Africa.'

Alem struggled to keep up with him and got the gist of it. 'So where do you come from?'

'I is an Ethiopian that happens to be born in England.'

Robert jumped into the conversation. 'I told you he had some connection with Ethiopia! You see, it's his mum and dad.'

'So your mother and father come from Ethiopia?' Alem asked.

'No, I mother and father is Jamaican and I is a

Rasta, you know. Ethiopia is our spiritual homeland, the land of Rastafari, God's country.'

'So you're not really Ethiopian!' Robert asked, feeling a little let down.

'I am really Ethiopian,' Asher replied, confusing Robert even more, 'really, really Ethiopian, I just happen to be born in England.' He turned to Alem. 'Alem, my man, do you know Shashamene?'

'Yes, I've never been there but I've heard of it.'

'That's where I want to go one day. I know it's not perfect but my journey through Africa must start there.'

'Where's Shashamene?' Robert asked, not wanting to be left out.

'Well,' Asher said, pointing to the carved shape of Africa hanging from his neck, 'Shashamene is the land given to all Rastafarians by Emperor Haile Selassie the first, so that we can return to the motherland and help to rebuild the great continent of Africa.'

Robert was intrigued. 'So when are these Rastas going then?'

'They gone already,' Asher said, almost leaping out of his seat, 'and they keep going. But hey, many now go to other parts of Africa as well. You want a drink?'

Alem and Robert asked for colas. As soon as Asher was back in his seat, he continued. 'The thing is, Africa has been divided up by the Europeans, you know, the slave drivers and the colonisers, so we say

Africa must unite. Without uniting, Africa will continue to be exploited by Babylon, so we want to unite Africa.'

'Yes, but look at all the wars. Look at Alem – tell him why you're here, Alem?'

Alem gave Asher a quick outline of his story. This time he included how he had arrived in Datchet, which surprised Robert.

Asher listened carefully and let him finish before responding. 'I know where you're coming from, brother. We don't support any kind of tribalism, we deal with one love.'

Soon they finished their drinks and were saying goodbye. 'Remember,' Asher said on the doorstep, 'this is I house and this is I bell, you can check I any time.'

Alem felt he had met a genuine friend and someone who had an interest in and an understanding of what he was going through. 'I like him,' he said to Robert as they walked up Romford Road.

'He's cool,' said Robert casually. 'He lives on his own, he studies hard and he never hurts anyone. I told you, he hates nobody, he's like you.'

As they stood outside Alem's house, Robert startled Alem with another one of his great ideas. 'I know – on Saturday, let's go out on our bikes. I'll take you to Beckton, guy, there's this cycle path there that goes on for miles.'

'OK,' Alem replied. 'What time shall we leave?'

'I'll come for you about eleven. Best if we try to get back before it gets too dark.'

'Fine.'

'I'll see you at school tomorrow anyway, but don't forget now,' Robert said, walking away. He turned around and began to walk backwards. 'So you like Asher then?'

'Yes, he's different.'

'But is he an Ethiopian?'

'Well, he makes some interesting points and he feels African.'

'Ah,' Robert interrupted, 'he says he's African and all Black people come from Africa, right?'

'That's right,' said Alem.

'Well, if you look at it another way, all human life started in Africa, so I'm an African too,' he said, laughing. 'I'm an African that just happens to be born in Manor Park. I'll see you tomorrow.'

'I'll see you, brother,' Alem shouted as he closed the gate.

CHAPTER 16

~ Guess Who's Coming to Dinner? ~

That Saturday Alem enjoyed his longest bike journey yet. Robert turned up at eleven as promised and they made their way to Beckton in the busy Saturday morning traffic. They connected with the cycle path at a place called Beckton Alps. It was an old slagheap that formed a large hill that had been converted for use as an artificial ski-slope. The path was called the Greenway and underneath it ran a sewer that went right into central London. In the summer it would stink but on cold days such as this one the only clue that gave away the filthy slime underneath was rising steam that could be seen seeping from the manhole covers.

Every few hundred yards they would stop to get through barriers that were built to allow only pedestrians, bikes and prams through. The path was surprisingly empty; they saw only a few old ladies walking small dogs, a few macho men walking big dogs and a couple of bikers and joggers.

It wasn't very long before they reached Bow. 'This is Bow,' Robert said as if he had reached some place of great significance.

Alem looked around him to see if he was missing something. 'What happens here?' he asked.

'Nothing,' Robert replied. 'There's just a big fly-over – we can carry on, we can go back up the path or we can make our way back on the streets.'

Alem opted for the streets, so Robert took him on a long trip through Stratford, Leyton and Forest Gate before returning to Manor Park. It was only three-thirty but Alem felt that he had experienced another great day. On the pavement at the corner of Romford and Meanly Roads they parted, with Alem politely saying thank you and Robert raving about how much better it was in the summer.

'See ya later,' Robert said and he rode away.

Alem turned his bike around to head down his road when two boys suddenly blocked him. 'Get off the bike,' one of the boys growled.

At first Alem thought they were upset with him for riding on the pavement. 'I'm going to ride on the road,' he said.

The same boy responded, 'You ain't going nowhere, you pussy! Get off the bike.'

'No, I will go now. I am sorry if—'

Alem didn't have the chance to finish. The boy who hadn't spoken pushed him off the bike and snatched it from him as he was falling. He tried to get up and grab the bike but the boy who had been

192

growling at him just growled again. 'Stay down, you stupid boy,' he said, tripping Alem over.

Fearful that they would start kicking him, Alem curled up into a ball and within seconds they were gone. Alem stayed curled up on the cold concrete until he felt a hand touching his shoulder. He began to straighten his body out and open his eyes.

Kneeling over him he saw a middle-aged woman. 'Shall we call the police?' she said, rubbing his shoulder.

'They deserve to go to prison,' said another voice.

Alem looked to his left, where another woman was standing looking down at him.

'No, I'm OK,' he said, trying to stand up.

'Are you sure?' said the first woman, who was now brushing him down.

'I'm OK,' Alem insisted politely.

'If you ask me, they should bring back hanging,' said the woman who was standing. 'How can you be on the streets and someone just come and tek your bike? What kind of world is this?'

'I'll be OK,' Alem said, now fully standing. 'I would like to thank you both.'

'It's all right, you go now,' said the first woman.

'And when you get home, you mek sure that your mother calls de police,' the second woman said. 'It's a damn disgrace!'

The short walk down Meanly Road was a long one. Alem walked slowly, head down and hands in pockets. He just couldn't believe how a good day had turned so bad so quickly.

Inside the house Mrs Fitzgerald went crazy. 'They must not get away with it! We must call the police!'

'No,' Alem said. 'Please don't call the police. I don't want any trouble.'

'I don't want any trouble,' Mrs Fitzgerald replied. 'When they took your bike away, that was trouble and the police are there to deal with trouble, so call the police,' she said, looking towards Mr Fitzgerald.

Mr Fitzgerald picked up the phone and was just about to speak when Alem raised his voice. 'You gave me the money and I bought that bike. I thank you very much for that but it is my bike and I don't want to call the police.'

Mr Fitzgerald put down the receiver and said, 'Well, I suppose it's up to you. But what's the problem? Do you know the boys that did it?'

'No, I don't know them. I have never seen them before.'

'But why,' Mrs Fitzgerald asked. 'Why don't you want to call the police?'

'I just want to forget it. If I want another bike I will get one but now I just want to rest. These boys will not be happy, something will happen to them.' Alem began to head towards his bedroom.

'What did they look like?' Mrs Fitzgerald asked.

'I didn't get a good look at them. One was Black and one was Asian.'

'Didn't anyone come and help you?' asked Mrs Fitzgerald.

'Yes,' replied Alem. 'Two women came to help me. I had a good look at them, one was Black and one was Asian as well.' He then made his way to his bedroom, turned his computer on and fell asleep on his bed.

Alem slept the kind of light sleep that meant he could hear noises from the house and still stay sleeping. He had fallen into bed wearing his jacket and shoes, and had chosen to sleep more as an attempt to forget everything than because of tiredness. At various times he heard Ruth in the house, he heard the bell ring a couple of times, he heard general communication coming from downstairs and at one point he even heard Mrs Fitzgerald telling someone to be quiet because he was sleeping. But he tried to block it all out. He was just about to fall into a deep sleep but then he could feel the presence of someone else in the room.

The person sat on the bed and put her hands over his eyes. 'Alem,' she said. It was Ruth. 'Alem, I'm sorry to hear about your bike. But listen, I have a surprise for you. I want you to keep your eyes closed, turn around slowly and then when I take my hands away you can open your eyes, all right?'

Alem wasn't in the mood for fun and games but he guessed that somehow his bike had been returned or a replacement bike had been obtained. 'OK,' he said almost reluctantly.

He turned around to face the door and sat up with Ruth's hands still covering his eyes. Ruth now pressed her hands against his eyes, making him feel slightly uncomfortable, and he felt she was doing this more for herself than for him.

'Open your eyes after three,' she said, pointing his head in the direction of the door and placing herself out of view. 'One – two – three!' She took her hands away and in a flash Alem's world lit up.

Standing before him was his father. His arms were outstretched and his smile said, Come and get me! Alem leaped from the bed straight into his arms. He hugged him hard, speaking to him in Amharic.

His father rubbed the top of his head with his hand and said, 'English, young man, you must speak English.' At which point they both burst into laughter and hugged some more, swinging each other from side to side.

Alem didn't notice all the other people standing just inside his room behind his father. It wasn't until his father properly entered the room that he noticed them disappearing downstairs: Mr and Mrs Fitzgerald, Mariam and Pamela from the Refugee Council, and Sheila the social worker. Ruth was the last to leave, carefully closing the door behind her.

His father looked around the room, noticing the picture on the computer. 'Very clever, very clever indeed! Your mother – I don't have a single picture of her. Do you still have the original?'

'Yes, Father.'

'You have a nice room here, young man. So you know how to use this computer then?'

'Yes, Father, I'm not great but I'm getting better.'

'And have you read all those books?' he said looking at all the books on the floor.

'No, not really.'

'What does "not really" mean?'

'Well, Father, I have read some of them but I have only read little parts of most of them.'

'If you start something, you must see it through.'

'I know, Father, I try,' Alem said cheekily, 'but there are so many things to see through.'

Alem's father sat with Alem on his bed and explained that he had landed at Heathrow Airport that morning. Then he made his way to central London on the Underground and contacted the Refugee Council. Not wanting to sadden the occasion too much, he only spoke a little about the way the war was impacting on the people. Alem knew that soon they had to talk about his mother but now he wanted to celebrate.

'Do you plan to go back?' Alem asked.

'No, of course not,' replied Mr Kelo. 'Not now anyway. I told you in my letter that at the moment there is nothing back there for me, so I come here. Let us go downstairs.'

They went downstairs to the living room to find that the other visitors had gone, leaving only the Fitzgerald family. 'Where have they all gone?' Mr Kelo asked Mr Fitzgerald, who was sitting next to Mrs Fitzgerald on the settee.

'They said that they felt it was best if they left. But Mariam – you know, the young girl – said she'll pick you up at ten tonight.'

Ruth took a brown envelope from the table. 'And she told me to give you this,' she said, handing it to him.

'What is this?' asked Mr Kelo.

'She said it was your money, your dollars turned into pounds or something like that.'

'Oh, yes,' Mr Kelo said, smiling and opening the envelope. There was a small amount of money inside, which he took out and waved as if it was thousands of pounds. 'I would like to take you all out for a treat,' he said.

Mr and Mrs Fitzgerald looked at each other, knowing that the amount he was waving around wasn't the kind of money that could give five people a treat, and anyway they weren't the type of people who ate out. They liked their own toilet, home cooking and home entertainment.

Ruth jumped up. 'Mr Kelo, we're fine. You only have until ten and it's seven now. You take Alem out, it's your night.'

'That's right,' Mrs Fitzgerald said with Mr Fitzgerald nodding in agreement.

'Are you sure?' Mr Kelo asked, looking around the room. All of them nodded. 'And Alem, what do you think?'

'Yes, Father, if it's OK with everyone else it's OK with me.'

'No, Alem,' said his father, encouraging Alem to think for himself. 'Never mind everyone else, I'm asking you. Is it OK with you?'

'Yes, Father.'

'All right, let's go.'

Alem still had his jacket on. He began to button it up quickly.

His father watched him and could see the sheer excitement on his face, as did the Fitzgeralds. All smiled at seeing him as happy as he had ever been.

'So what do you want to eat?' asked Mr Kelo. That devious look returned to his face. 'Remember we are in London, you can eat anything here.' He paused. 'Let me guess – Italian!'

'No,' said Alem with an even more devious look on his face. 'Ethiopian.'

They called a taxi and went to the Merkato, an

Ethiopian restaurant that Ruth had discovered on Plashet Road. They ate traditional fairsolia beans and doro wot sauce on injera, a large bread made from flour and water, and to remind themselves of home they performed gursha, feeding each other with their hands. The other customers (all Europeans) watched them feeding each other while trying not to be openly nosy. Alem and his father carried on regardless.

When they had finished eating, they talked for a while. 'I want you to be absolutely honest,' Mr Kelo said sternly. 'How do you find this family?'

'Father, I don't have one complaint. They have given me a nice home; they don't pressure me in any way. They let me do what I want but they are always ready to talk to me and they treat me very good. I can't say anything bad about them.'

'And your school?'

'My school is good. There are children from all over the world there and the teachers are good. It is very different from school back home but I like it very much and I have made good friends there.'

'Oh, yes,' Mr Kelo replied, 'and who is Robert?'

'Robert is my good friend, he's a nice boy. I met him by accident on my first day and he was the one to show me around the school and help me fit in. The problem is he smokes.'

'He smokes?'

'Yes,' Alem replied. 'Many children smoke here, no

one really says anything.'

Mr Kelo leaned forward over the table. 'Do you smoke?' he said.

'Of course not,' Alem said. 'I can't see its purpose.'

After the meal they caught a taxi back to the house where Mariam was waiting to take Mr Kelo to a bed-and-breakfast.

'What will you do tomorrow?' Mr Fitzgerald asked.

'Tomorrow I have a meeting with the Refugee Council in the morning, then on Monday morning I will have to report to the Home Office to make my application for political asylum. So I will see you all late afternoon, if I may.'

Everybody agreed.

'I'll call you tomorrow to see how you are, and if it's OK with you I'll see you after school on Monday,' he said to Alem.

'Yes, Father,' Alem replied. He walked towards him and hugged him.

As they were leaving, Mrs Fitzgerald said, 'On Monday we would like to feed you, Mr Kelo.'

'Thank you,' he replied.

Alem said, 'Can I help you cook, Mrs Fitzgerald?'

'Of course you can. If you like, you can do the cooking, we'll just help you.'

'Right, Father, that's it, on Monday I'll feed you.'

Mr Kelo reached out and rubbed Alem's jaw. 'OK, young man, I look forward to that.'

CHAPTER 17

~ Campsfield ~

After school on Monday, Alem ran home as fast as he could to cook his father's meal.

'Did you get the spaghetti?' he asked Mrs Fitzgerald as he hung up his jacket and went into the kitchen.

'Yes, I got it,' she replied.

'And is it Italian?'

'Yes.'

'Actually made in Italy?'

'Yes, yes, yes! It says "produce of Italy" on the packet and the shopkeeper said he knows the Italian family who export it.' She handed him the packet. 'You can't get more Italian than that. Now wash your hands.'

Mrs Fitzgerald guided him around the kitchen and helped him prepare the spaghetti and the sauce. Ruth came home as the cooking was ending and laid the table for them before going to her room to listen to some music. Not sure exactly what time Mr Kelo was coming, the household went into a state of limbo. Mr Fitzgerald was happily rearranging things in the garden shed, Mrs Fitzgerald began washing used pots and cleaning the kitchen, and Alem went upstairs and started to tidy his room.

Then the doorbell rang and everybody headed for the front door. Alem leaped down the stairs and beat everyone to it. He opened the door to find Mariam and Sheila standing there. He looked beyond them and to the left of them and to the right of them, hoping that there was a surprise or a trick in store, but he could see by the expressions on their faces that they were playing no games.

'Where's my father?' Alem asked.

Mrs Fitzgerald came up behind Alem. 'Let them come in, Alem.'

They all went into the living room without saying a word until Mariam spoke. She directed her words to Alem. 'I went with your father today to the Home Office to help him with his application and he was arrested and taken to Campsfield.'

No one spoke. Alem stared at her. He felt like crying, he felt like shouting, but instead he just whispered, 'What is Campsfield?'

'Campsfield is a detention centre where they detain asylum seekers.'

'You mean it's a prison?' Alem asked.

'Well, officially it's not a prison,' Mariam replied, 'however, I'm afraid that everyone I've known who's been there has said it's just like a prison.'

'What can we do?' said Ruth.

'There's not much we can do,' Mariam said. 'We'll be using Nicholas Morgan again, Alem's barrister. He'll get to work first thing tomorrow. Until then there really is very little that can be done.'

Sheila reminded Alem that she was there if he needed her. Alem thanked them both and went to his room. He felt as if his life was a roller-coaster going from one extreme to the other. He considered his age and asked himself if this was the way his life would continue. He sat silently. He heard Sheila and Mariam leave. He heard the Fitzgeralds talking; he had no intention of joining them.

When Mrs Fitzgerald stood outside his door urging him to eat something before the food went cold, he just said, 'I can't eat now, Mrs Fitzgerald.'

As the Fitzgeralds were eating, he went to the bathroom, but after that he never left his room for the rest of the night.

The next morning to everyone's surprise Alem was up early. He had breakfast as usual and went to school. Mrs Fitzgerald tried to get him to stay home but he insisted on going, saying that he had to learn as much as he could. But at school everyone could see that something was wrong with him. Robert knew it was serious but instead of asking, he hoped that Alem would tell him what it was.

Alem walked home alone and when he arrived, Mrs Fitzgerald, who was in the middle of a phone conversation, opened the door. 'Alem has just come in now,' she said to the person on the phone. 'Would you like to speak to him? OK, here he is,' she said, handing him the phone.

'Hello. This is Nicholas Morgan here, Alem.'

'Hello,' Alem replied.

'Look,' Nicholas continued, 'I don't want you to get too worried. We're going to apply for bail. He really doesn't have to be in there and we think that we have a strong case. So don't worry too much, all right?'

'All right,' Alem said.

'I'll let you know what's happening as soon as I know anything. Now can you put Mrs Fitzgerald back on?'

'Yes,' said Alem. He handed the phone back to Mrs Fitzgerald.

'OK,' she said. 'OK – will do – no problem – thank you – goodbye,' and she put the phone down. 'Don't worry, son,' she said to Alem.

'I'm all right,' Alem replied. He went to his room, turned on his computer and changed his clothes.

He didn't say much but he ate with the family as normal that evening, retiring to his room early again. Soon after there was a knock on the door.

It was Ruth.

'Can I come in?' she said, opening the door ever so slightly.

'Of course.'

She entered the room and sat on the bed next to Alem. 'I really don't know what to say. If I were in your place, I would have cracked up by now. You've had to deal with so much.'

'I suppose it's my life so I have to deal with it.'

'I don't think it's as simple as that. You have to be tough.' She had a small package in her hand which she handed to Alem. 'I have a present for you. I took a chance – you may hate them but I thought I'd give it a try.'

Alem took the gifts from her. They were in a brown paper bag. He held it at one end and let the gifts fall into the other hand. It was two CDs, one of Eritrean traditional music and one of Ethiopian traditional music. The minute beginnings of a smile appeared on Alem's face.

'There is a problem,' he said mock seriously. 'You didn't get me any Tigrean music nor any Somalian music.'

'Gosh, Alem, I don't know the difference. I'll take them back if you don't like them,' Ruth said, holding her hand out.

'Only joking, silly,' Alem said, holding the CDs to his chest. 'They're great.'

Ruth rolled her eyes and smiled. 'I looked hard for

those. I was trying to find an Ethiopian band but I couldn't find any.'

After Ruth left the room, Alem went to his computer and played the CDs. He had never been interested in music and he certainly was not the type to listen to traditional music, but this was different. The recording quality was basic, as if recorded in a field or by someone simply placing a microphone in front of the musicians. It didn't have the clean, polished sound of a studio recording but it had a profound effect on Alem. The stringed instruments, the drumming and most of all the chanting meant that he was hearing the sounds of home. These were the birth songs, the death songs, the wedding songs and the love songs that he had for so long taken for granted. He closed his eyes and drifted from the Ethiopian town of Harar to the Eritrean city of Asmara; then he drifted into sleep.

There was a knock on the door. Alem woke up. It was Mrs Fitzgerald. 'Alem, maybe you should get in bed now, it's almost midnight.'

Alem couldn't believe he had been asleep so long. 'Yes, Mrs Fitzgerald. I'm sorry, I fell asleep.'

The next time Alem woke up it was morning. The sound of pop music was blaring out from Ruth's room as she was busy getting ready for work. Before she left, Alem caught her on the landing and thanked her for the CDs again. 'I don't know what you were thinking but all I can say is that it was just what I needed.'

His mood that day at school was a bit better and he managed to explain to Robert and Buck what had happened, how his father came and how he went.

'We have to do something,' Robert said. 'It's not fair!'

'There's nothing we can do now,' Alem replied.

When Alem arrived home, Mrs Fitzgerald had a message for him. She told him to go and get changed and then to wait in the living room. Alem just didn't know what to expect but the seriousness of her tone made him very worried. She came into the living room and sat opposite Alem.

'Well, Nicholas Morgan has been on the phone to me again today and he sounded hopeful. Tomorrow morning your father will appear in court and Nicholas will be making an application for bail on his behalf. He thinks that there's a good chance that bail will be granted but he said he couldn't be one hundred per cent sure.'

Alem didn't know how to take the news, he wasn't sure whether it was good or bad.

'Do I have to go to court as well?' he asked.

'Nicholas said no. He said that we don't want to be seen taking you out of school for this and that he will have your file with him anyway because it may help your father's case.'

'So I just carry on as normal?'

'That's just what he said,' Mrs Fitzgerald replied. 'It's going to be difficult waiting for the results of the hearing but Nicholas does know his business.'

Alem looked her in the eye and said, 'I'm sorry for being such a problem.'

Mrs Fitzgerald rose to her feet. 'Nonsense!' she said. 'The only problem I have is you thinking you're a problem. Now stop saying sorry and stop saying problem, will you?' She looked down at him most seriously but then quickly winked at him.

Alem smiled. 'Yes, Mrs Fitzgerald.'

'And Alem?'

'Yes, Mrs Fitzgerald?'

'Remember, there's a lot of people who love you.'

'Yes, Mrs Fitzgerald.'

CHAPTER 18

~ Real Men Cry ~

At dinnertime the next day after Alem and Robert had visited the chip shop, Alem stopped at a phone box to phone home. He had told Robert about the hearing so Robert knew how important the call could be as he waited outside.

Mrs Fitzgerald answered the phone. 'Hello?'

'Hello, Mrs Fitzgerald.'

'Hello, Alem.'

'Have you heard from the court yet?'

'Nicholas has just rung here.'

'What did he say?'

'He said your father is on his way here.'

'You mean they've let him out?'

'That's right, he's free and I think he'll be here before you get here. So go back to school and don't worry.'

'Yes, Mrs Fitzgerald.'

'Goodbye.'

'Goodbye.'

Robert could see that the news was good. 'They let him out then?'

'Yes,' Alem said, 'he's already on his way here.'

The afternoon just couldn't go quickly enough for Alem. He was counting every minute down and he struggled to concentrate on his work. When he got home there was another emotional reunion, but Alem could see that the detention centre had had a negative effect on his father. He looked extremely tired and nervous. Mariam and Pamela were with him and as they all sat in the living room, Pamela began to speak.

'We won a battle but we haven't won the war.'

Alem and his father looked at each other. They hated the war metaphor.

Pamela noticed their reaction.

'I'm sorry for using such an unfortunate phrase but you know what I mean. We still have a long way to go. Today the courts have agreed that your father's hearing and yours,' she said, looking at Alem, 'should be combined, so the same adjudicator can hear both your cases. Your father will now be in court with you on 15th February, which isn't very far away – twenty days to be exact.'

'But what will Mr Kelo do until then?' asked Mr Fitzgerald, who was standing by the door.

'Well,' Pamela continued, 'he can't work. He can get a little state help – and I mean a little – and Sheila has fixed him up with a hotel. It's not great but it's somewhere, and it's not very far from here.'

'Can't he stay with us?' said Mr Fitzgerald.

'Sheila reckons it might complicate things,' Mariam said. 'Apparently if the make-up of the household changes, the condition of the fostering may be invalid.'

Alem knew it wasn't perfect but he also knew that things could have been much worse. 'Where is this hotel?' he asked Pamela.

'Well . . .' she hesitated. 'It's called a hotel but these hotels are full of homeless families and asylum seekers. It's not like a Holiday Inn or even like the nice little place you stayed at in Datchet. It's a bit rough, to say the least. It's at the Forest Gate end of Romford Road, so it's not far at all.'

'I think we should go now,' Mariam said. 'We have to buy a few things and get Mr Kelo checked into his new home.' She handed Alem a business card. 'That's the name and address of the hotel.'

Alem took it, and read it. 'Father, can I come to see you tomorrow after school?'

'No,' his father said to everyone's surprise. 'Give me a couple of days to sort some things out and to talk to my barrister and then come. Why don't you come on Saturday? You'll have more time.'

'OK,' Alem said. His father's reasoning made sense to him.

On Friday night Mr Kelo rang Alem at home. 'How are you, young man?' he asked.

'Everything is fine, Father.'

'So are you coming tomorrow?'

'Yes, Father.'

'Why don't you come early, like nine o'clock? We could go shopping together.'

'Yes, Father, I would like that.'

The next morning Alem walked down Romford Road, remembering the last time he had ventured down there. He feared that he might meet the people who took his bike and at the same time he looked at every bike that passed, trying to see if it was his. He arrived at the Hartman Hotel at exactly nine and walked into the building looking for the reception. He couldn't find it. As he stood trying to look for any signs that would point him to the reception desk, people passed him going in and going out but no one offered to help him. Then he saw someone looking at him as he was trying to find his way. The man stood silently watching at the bottom of the stairs. He was about eighteen, dressed in jeans and a heavy leather coat, and looked Arab or Mediterranean.

He approached Alem. 'What are you looking for?' he asked, expressionless.

'I am looking for my father,' Alem replied.

'What room is he in?'

'I don't know.'

Alem could see him thinking.

'Did he come in about two days ago, tall man, on his own?'

'Yes, yes, that sounds like him,' Alem replied, cheering up.

'I think he is on the top floor at the back.'

'Do you know what the room number is?' Alem asked.

'There are no numbers on the room doors. But I'm sure I saw him moving into that room.'

Alem climbed the four flights of stairs and at the top there were four doors. Two were facing the front of the building and two were facing the back. He stood for a moment wondering which door could be his father's. Then he heard sounds coming from one. Putting his head to the door, and he could hear children playing and adults talking. That made things easier for him. He knocked on the other door and his father opened it.

'Hello, Father,' he said, noticing the flaking paint on the door.

His father noticed him noticing the paintwork. He smiled. 'It's not the Holiday Inn and it's not the Palace Hotel, as our friend said, it's a bit rough.'

Alem entered the room and took an instant dislike to the place. The cheap carpet was so worn in places that the underlay was showing. There were areas of the wall where the wallpaper had peeled off, leaving patches of damp plaster. The curtains moved as the wind blew outside. Two panes of glass were completely missing and had been replaced with pieces of cardboard. The only bits of furniture in the room were a single bed, two hard pink chairs, a small table and a wardrobe. The only luxury was a radio, almost covering the small table it rested on. Alem was horrified.

'Father, you can't live here!'

'I have no choice, young man.'

'But Father, look at it – and it stinks!'

'Well, I will have to try my best to stop it from stinking,' he said as if he was happy to take on the task.

'Father, there must be somewhere else for you to go. I will talk to Sheila for you, I'm sure she can find you somewhere else.'

Mr Kelo grabbed one of the pink chairs and turned it around so it was opposite the other chair. 'Sit down, I want to talk to you,' he said to Alem, pointing to the seat.

Alem sat down and Mr Kelo sat down facing him. 'You have lost your mother, I have lost my wife. We are far away from home. Our lives are changing. Things will never be as they were and things will not stay as they are. We are both lucky to be here. We know that, don't we?'

Alem nodded his head.

'We know what war is like,' Mr Kelo continued. 'Let us not be ungrateful and let us not be greedy. If we are patient, things will work out. This is a good country and everybody has to start somewhere.'

'I know you are right, Father,' Alem said quietly, 'but I just don't like to think of you living here. I feel bad because I live in a better place than you.'

'Don't worry, this won't be for long.'

'OK, Father.'

Alem paused for what seemed quite a long time. His father watched him look around the room but then he looked his father in his eyes in a way his father had never seen before.

'Father, how did Mother die?'

His father looked nervous. He hesitated before speaking. 'Well, let me put it like this, young man, I wasn't there but I know it was a violent death. Sometimes it's best not to know the details of these things. I have to tell you, son, that the night I found out about her death I cried all night, and then when I tried to go out the next day I couldn't. Every time I saw a woman, I looked to see if it was your mother. I could not believe that we had lost her. I had to return home, I could not face the day, and when I was home I cried even more. I had to lock myself away for a week just to cry.'

Mr Kelo's eyes started to water. Alem had never seen him like this and Mr Kelo was aware of this. 'Let me tell you something, young man,' he continued, 'real men cry, real men have feelings. Any man that lives without emotions or feelings is not a real man. These people that kill and think nothing of it are cowards. Real men feel, real men cry.'

Alem's eyes began to water. He reached out both his hands and they held each other's hands as Alem wept quietly. As Alem spoke, the tears rolled down his face and over his lips. 'I didn't even say goodbye to her.'

'None of us did, and she would understand why. We never knew the plans of those evil people.'

'Father, do we all do evil?'

His father thought for a while. 'We all make mistakes and we are all capable of evil but I must tell you young man, I met your mother when she was fourteen years old and I have never known her to say an evil word or do an evil deed. Not once. Do you know whose idea EAST was?'

'Yours,' Alem replied.

'No, young man, it was your mother's. She was the one who said to me and my friend Asfa that we should start an organisation to bring people together. She was the one with the vision, she was the one who was not prepared to sit back and watch us tear ourselves apart.'

Alem sat back, lifted up his chest and took in a long, deep breath. 'I know what I must do, Father,' he said, still looking into his father's eyes. 'I must represent Mother's ideas, I should promote her dream.'

His father smiled. 'You got it, young man! You do that and that will mean that she lives. Now,' he said, standing up, 'I'm told that I will get some financial help next week. My money is running out but I have enough to get some food for the time being. So let's go shopping.'

They took a bus and went to a large supermarket. Mr Kelo was choosing mainly vegetables and tinned meat products. As Alem pushed the trolley he began to ask himself questions, and when he felt that he couldn't answer them himself, he asked his father.

'Father, why are you buying so many things in cans? You don't like canned food.'

'Well, young man, there is nowhere to store fresh meat in that place so if I want meat it will have to be canned.'

'And Father, you don't have anywhere to cook, do you?'

'Yes, you didn't see it but there is a place for cooking there. It's downstairs and . . .' He hesitated. 'It's a bit rough.'

At the checkout point Mr Kelo was paying the cashier while Alem was packing the carrier bags. When he looked over to another checkout in the distance, he saw a face that he recognised. For a moment he couldn't remember where from, then it came to him; it was the man in the hotel who had directed him to his father's room. He still looked glum. Alem tried to catch his attention by waving to him but the man didn't see him.

'Who are you waving to?' Alem's father asked, joining in with the packing.

'That man over there. I met him this morning in the hotel.'

'Oh yes, I have seen him there too. I think he lives downstairs somewhere. You'll see him again, I'm sure.'

When they got back to the hotel, Alem had an even bigger shock when he saw the kitchen. It was a communal cooking area between the communal toilet and the communal bathroom on the second floor. The walls were covered in damp, there was no storage space, only the tiniest of sinks, and the gas cooker was a survivor from the 1970s that had turned black and brown with spilt and burnt food.

Alem's father looked at Alem and said, 'That used to be white.'

Alem looked horrified.

'Don't say anything,' said Mr Kelo. 'Let's go and put the food away.'

'Where?'

'I'll show you.'

He led Alem up to his room and opened his wardrobe. Inside hung the few items of clothing that Mr Kelo possessed. At the bottom of the wardrobe Alem saw two small pots and a box containing a couple of cans of baked beans and half a large onion.

Mr Kelo ran his hands over Alem's head. 'It's a bit rough,' he said smiling. Alem knew that his father was willing to endure the hardship and that nothing that he could say would change things.

'Yes,' he said, smiling back at his father, 'it's a bit rough.'

Later that afternoon Alem and his father waited their turn to use the kitchen and then cooked some boiled rice, corned beef and vegetables. Alem hated the meal, as did his father, but they both felt it was their duty not to show it.

After the meal Alem walked home relatively happy. It felt strange saying goodbye to his father and walking home to another family; it was as if his father had also become a friend. It was even stranger when Mr Kelo rang Alem on Sunday evening to find that Alem was inviting him to the Fitzgeralds for a meal.

'Remember,' Alem said, 'I owe you some Italian spaghetti.'

And so it was that on Monday evening Mr Kelo ate at Meanly Road, spaghetti bolognese prepared by Alem with a little help from Mrs Fitzgerald and Ruth. On Tuesday after school Alem headed straight to the hotel, where he had a stir-fry cooked by his father, and on Wednesday Mr Kelo was back at the Fitzgeralds'.

All the Fitzgeralds loved watching the Kelos build their relationship back up and they encouraged Alem to see his father as much as he could. Robert could see a big change in Alem; he walked and talked more confidently and he worked even more diligently, although it was obvious that he was missing his mother and he was continually thinking about Africa and war.

After the Wednesday-night meal, Mr Fitzgerald stood up at the table and gave what amounted to an after-dinner speech. 'Alem is a great boy. We have had many children here over the years but I can honestly say that none have been as good as Alem. Don't get me wrong, they haven't all been bad children, but none have been as hard-working and well-mannered as Alem. Since he's been in this house, we haven't had one reason to tell him off, he's even better behaved than my fish. I could say that his room could be a bit tidier but at least he reads the books, and anyway the fish ain't got any books.'

Everyone laughed and Mr Kelo looked at Alem with pride.

'We have had some sad times,' Mr Fitzgerald continued. 'When Mrs Kelo was killed we thought that we had lost a piece of our own family, but Alem is a strong boy. And now it is great to see you both together. That's all I want to say really.' He stopped for a while and thought. 'Oh yes, I remember,' he said, picking up an envelope that was under his side plate, 'we want to give you this, a little present from us.' He handed the envelope to Mr Kelo, who opened it immediately.

'Thank you, Mr Fitzgerald,' Mr Kelo replied. 'Thank you all! Alem, look, they are tickets for the Millennium Dome.'

'The Millennium Dome!' said Alem. 'I've heard so much about it, it's always on the television. Thank you, Mr Fitzgerald.'

'I just hope you haven't got anything planned for Saturday,' said Mr Fitzgerald, uttering a sigh of relief as he sat down after all the excitement.

On Saturday Alem and his father travelled by train to the Dome. Alem was cold but his father was feeling it the most; he had not really acclimatised and it was a particularly cold day. Alem wasn't impressed with the architecture of the Dome but he liked its size, and the displays and the interactive installations amused him. Most of all he was just happy to be sightseeing with his father once more.

When they left the Dome late in the afternoon, Mr Kelo said that he wanted to take Alem somewhere else. They got on the Underground train and made their way to Seven Sisters station in north London. After leaving the station they walked for about two hundred yards to what looked like a shop.

'Do you know what this place is?' Mr Kelo asked Alem.

'No.'

'This is the office of EAST,' he said, pressing the bell.

The door was opened by a man in his forties who greeted them in Amharic and waved them in. Inside, the room was full of people, either Ethiopians or Eritreans. They were talking and joking. Alem's father shook hands with all of them, showing off his son at the same time. The walls were covered with posters depicting scenes from Somalia, Kenya, Sudan, Ethiopia and Eritrea. Many of them looked as if they had been up there for years. Some of them were straight from the office of tourism. 'Come to Ethiopia, 13 months of sunshine,' said one, showing a tribal woman carrying a basket on her head.

Within fifteen minutes of arriving, Mr Kelo was saying goodbye to everyone. On their way back to the station he told Alem, 'The only reason why I brought you here today was to show you our only surviving office and just to show you some Ethiopians and Eritreans who are getting along fine. Peace is possible and peace will happen; the thing is, we want it now. Some people want it but will not do anything about achieving it. We already have what they call a United States of America. They may be debating what the coins will look like or what shape the cucumbers will be, but they are also creating a United States of Europe. All we want is a United States of Africa but we realise that before we can unite a continent, we have to unite the regions. That's all we want. We are not a political party trying to make a government, we just want people to sing and dance together. We want peace, we want a united Africa.'

'Me too,' Alem said as they entered the Underground station and made their way back to east London.

CHAPTER 19

~ Court Again ~

Early on the morning of Tuesday 15th February, Mrs Fitzgerald picked up Mr Kelo in a taxi. From the hotel they went to Stratford station, where they caught the Underground train into central London. In the court Alem checked the list for their names and saw that they were to appear in the same courtroom in front of the adjudicator he had seen previously. They made their way to courtroom number nine; this time it was Alem who led the way. They sat on the same bench outside the courtroom next to a young Asian couple who were speaking to their barrister through an interpreter.

Just as the Asian couple were being taken into the court, Nicholas Morgan arrived. Tired but smiling, he apologised for being late. He had been dealing with another case in court four, which had run on longer than expected. As the three of them sat on the bench, Nicholas stayed standing and began to outline how he thought things would proceed.

'The adjudicator is seeing you for the second time,

Alem, and he is seeing you for the first time, Mr Kelo. Now that he is being asked to deal with you as a couple, I think he will request another adjournment to give us time to make a more detailed representation of your case, Mr Kelo, and to present you as a family, so to speak.'

'I understand,' said Mr Kelo.

'Do you think they will have to speak?' asked Mrs Fitzgerald.

'It is possible, but I don't think so; they will only have to confirm their names and addresses as normal. It will be pretty much like the last time but –' he was now addressing Alem and Mr Kelo – 'I may use the letter as evidence. The adjudicator already has a copy of the letter but it may have to be quoted.'

'I understand,' said Mr Kelo.

Alem and Mrs Fitzgerald just nodded their heads. They waited for a short while and soon the Tamil couple came out of the courtroom. Alem watched them as they walked away with their barrister and interpreter, trying to see their expressions. He thought that if they had a good result they would be happy and this could mean that the adjudicator was in a good mood. But their expressions were neutral, just as they had been when they went in, and Alem couldn't tell whether this was good, bad or just another adjournment.

They waited for another ten minutes, then the

same woman as before came and called for 'Case Number C651438'.

Nothing had changed in the courtroom and the moment he entered it, Alem felt guilty of something again. Mrs Fitzgerald sat alone in the family seating area and Alem and his father sat together in front of the adjudicator's seat. When the adjudicator walked in, Alem knew exactly what to do and he stood up quickly, quicker than anyone else in the courtroom, and when the adjudicator sat down, Alem sat on cue. The clerk announced the case number and identified the parties involved. For a couple of minutes the adjudicator read the papers in front of him.

He took off his glasses and looked at Alem. 'Oh yes, I remember you.' He put on his glasses and read a bit more before addressing the representatives.

'I take it you,' he said, addressing the state representative, 'are representing the Secretary of State on both cases?'

He confirmed this.

'And you – the adjudicator turned to Nicholas – 'are representing both appellants?'

'Yes,' Nicholas said confidently.

The adjudicator looked back towards the state representative again. 'Does the state have anything to add to that which was stated in the last hearing? I have your report and it seems very straightforward to me.'

The representative stood up. 'No, sir. There has not been an escalation of hostilities in Ethiopia and Eritrea. We recognise that fighting still continues but this fighting is confined to very small areas in both countries. Most of the people in Ethiopia and Eritrea have not seen any fighting whatsoever. In the opinion of the state, the risk to the lives of the appellants is minimal and we see no reason why they should not return to their country of origin and consider living in an area where they do not feel threatened.'

He sat down. Nicholas stood up and began to speak.

'The fact is, sir, that there has been a massive escalation of the fighting between both sides, and although the United Nations has appointed Algeria as mediator, both sides are refusing to come to the negotiating table. It may be true to say that most of the population of both countries will never see any fighting, but the people who live along the border and those that are living in cities within easy range of the opposing forces are being subjected to war every day. Furthermore, sir – and this is crucial to this case – my clients are not being persecuted because they are on one side or the other, they are being persecuted because they are on both sides. At this point in time there is no place for what is a mixed-race family in this conflict. When young Alem Kelo is in Ethiopia, he is persecuted because he is Eritrean, and when he is in Eritrea, he is persecuted because he is Ethiopian. This young man is in an impossible position and it is clear that the only way he could return to either country and live safely is when there is a genuine peace throughout the region.'

Nicholas searched some papers on the desk in front of him and picked one of them up. 'For this small family the matter of war is not academic. Since the last time Alem appeared in this court, his mother has been brutally murdered. Imagine how difficult it must have been for Mr Kelo to let his son know that his mother was found hacked to death.'

There was a thud and everyone in the courtroom turned to see what it was. Alem had collapsed in his seat and fallen forward. Even though he was already haunted by the death of his mother, it was the first time he had heard it being described as 'hacked to death'.

Mr Kelo tried to move him back into an upright position as the usher calmly asked, 'Would the young man like some water?'

'Yes, water, please,' said Mr Kelo.

The usher poured water from a jug and handed the glass to Alem's father, who poured water into his hand and began to flick it on to Alem's face. He shook him and Alem began to revive. Then he put the glass to his mouth and Alem drank slowly.

'Would the young man like to leave the

proceedings for a while?' said the adjudicator.

'Yes,' said Mr Kelo.

'No,' said Alem. He looked towards his father and whispered, 'I'm all right, Father, I want to stay.'

'Are you sure?' Mr Kelo asked, concerned. 'You can get some fresh air and then come back when you feel better.'

'No, I'll be all right, Father. I want to stay here with you and Mr Morgan.'

'Are you sure?'

'Yes.'

Mr Kelo turned to the adjudicator and said, 'He would like to stay.'

'Very well, please continue,' said the adjudicator.

Nicholas looked towards Mr Kelo, who signalled to him to continue. Nicholas cleared his throat and began to speak.

'Mr Kelo sent a letter from Eritrea to his son, a copy of which you should have before you. They are in fear of their lives, which is why Mr Kelo came to England. This is a family that is terrified, this is a family that cannot afford to take any more risks.'

Nicholas sat down while the adjudicator began to read again. He read for a long time, spreading the papers out in front of him and glancing up periodically. After a long silence he addressed Alem and his father.

'Could you stand, please? I have listened to both of

you very carefully and I have read all the papers concerning this case. One cannot but be moved by the death of Mrs Kelo and I offer my condolences. But you must also understand that I cannot make a judgement based on emotions, I have to look at the facts. The war between Ethiopia and Eritrea is a border dispute, some may call it a skirmish but at any rate it is not a full-out war. There are millions of Ethiopians and Eritreans who are not affected by the war, and there must be other families that consist of members from both communities, and the records show that they are not all making their way here. Now I want you both to listen very carefully, as it is very important that you fully understand what I am going to say. The circumstances of this case have drastically changed in the last few weeks. When this case first came to my attention last month, my major consideration was the wellbeing of the juvenile. Being separated from his country was one issue, but I believed that being separated from his family was a more important matter. But things are somewhat different now. Now that your family is reunited, albeit with one member missing, the issue of the juvenile not having anyone to return to and not having a legal guardian is no longer relevant.'

There was a pause and Alem and his father, Nicholas and Mrs Fitzgerald could sense that something was wrong.

'I have given this case much consideration,' the adjudicator continued, 'but I'm afraid that I must turn down your application for asylum.'

There was a gasp from Mrs Fitzgerald as she began to weep. Nicholas was completely taken by surprise and just didn't know where to look. Alem and his father just looked straight ahead in disbelief. Both of them tried to go over what he had said in their heads in case there was a misunderstanding.

Alem spoke from his seat to Nicholas. 'What does this mean?'

The adjudicator responded. 'It means that you must try and make a life with your father in your own country. It is possible. You now have your father with you so you will not be alone. Your barrister will explain. We do have a very fair system of justice here so you do have the right to appeal.'

The adjudicator stood up, as did everyone else in the court except Mrs Fitzgerald, and then he walked out.

Outside the courtroom Nicholas tried to soften the blow that all three had just received but it was easy to see that he had really not expected things to turn out this way. 'This is not the end of the line. We shall be lodging an appeal immediately. He just ignored so many of the facts before him. We have to get that judgement overturned.'

They listened impassively, thanked him and made

their way out of central London. Mr Kelo went with Alem and Mrs Fitzgerald to Meanly Road, where they told Mr Fitzgerald what had happened and phoned the Social Services and Mariam at the Refugee Council. By five o'clock when Ruth arrived home from work, the house was full. Mariam, Pamela, Sheila, Mr and Mrs Fitzgerald, Alem and his father were all crowded into the living room, talking quietly about the way things had gone in court and what could happen in the future. It was as if they were in mourning.

CHAPTER 20

~ This is Politics ~

Mrs Fitzgerald suggested that Alem should have a day off school but once more he was determined to go and his father agreed. So the next day Alem went to school, trying as much as possible to concentrate on his work and not to let his sadness show. But Robert was beginning to read Alem well; he knew something was wrong and he knew that Alem had gone to court the day before. So at dinnertime he asked him how things went at court and Alem told him everything.

Robert was shocked. 'Just run away,' he said. 'I'm serious, man! Don't go back if you don't want to, just run away. Did the judge know about your mum?'

'Yes,' Alem replied, 'but he said my father's alive and that he should look after me in our own country.'

'That's not right, guy, we got to do something,' Robert said, looking around the playground full of kids playing.

'We are, we are making another appeal.'

'No, we got to do something more than that.'

After school that afternoon Alem couldn't see

Robert so he walked home alone. But much later, when their evening meal was over and everyone at the Fitzgeralds' house was quietening down for the night, the doorbell rang. It was nine o'clock and they weren't expecting any visitors, so everyone was surprised.

'I'll get it,' Mr Fitzgerald shouted.

He opened the door to find three boys looking back at him. He recognised the first; it was Robert.

'Hello, Mr Fitzgerald. I'm sorry for disturbing you, especially 'cause it's quite late, but do you remember me? I'm Alem's friend, I met you not long ago.'

'Yes, I remember you,' he replied. He looked at the other two.

'Oh, this is Buck,' Robert said hastily, 'and this is Asher. Both friends of Alem. I know it's late, like, but could we please see Alem? It's very important and I promise that we won't stay long.'

It was raining. Mr Fitzgerald noticed that the boys were dressed as if they were out on a warm summer evening. They were soaking.

'Come in, wipe your feet and go in the living room. Alem,' he shouted upstairs as they made their way in, 'you have visitors!'

Alem jumped off his bed and ran downstairs as quickly as he could. It didn't occur to him that it could be Robert or any of his other friends; he was thinking social worker, barrister, father even.

'They're in the living room,' Mr Fitzgerald said, heading for the back room.

When Alem entered the living room he was surprised by what he saw and even more surprised by the condition of his visitors. 'What are you all doing here? Look at you, soaking!'

They were standing in a line in front of the window as if they were on an identification parade. 'We have to talk to you,' said Robert.

'Yes, we have to reason with you,' Asher added.

'OK,' said Alem, not sure what to expect. 'Sit down – no,' he said quickly, realising that Mrs Fitzgerald would not take kindly to any marks left by their wet bottoms. 'Don't sit, just stay where you are.'

'Dat's cool,' said Asher.

'We want to start a campaign,' said Robert.

'What?' Alem was not sure whether he had heard Robert properly.

'We want to start a campaign,' Robert repeated.

'What kind of campaign?'

'A campaign to keep you and your dad here, man,' Buck said lazily. 'This planet is for everyone, borders are for no one. It's all about freedom.'

'Yes,' said Asher, 'there ain't no justice, just us, so we will defend you. Your barrister and them – let them do their thing – but this is where it happens, man, on the streets.'

Buck continued. 'What we're saying is that you got

people working for you in the system, right – suits and educated people – but you need some people power, you know. Who's this judge anyway? He's just a human being, he ain't no better than us, so if we speak loud enough he will have to listen.'

Alem was overwhelmed by it all and a little lost for words. 'I don't know, I don't want to start any trouble.'

'You're in trouble already,' Robert said, with the others nodding in agreement.

'I don't know,' Alem said. 'I'll have to think about it and I'll have to ask my father what he thinks.'

'OK,' Robert said. 'I think we should go now, but listen, it's Thursday tomorrow, and we're going to have a meeting at the rehearsal cellar at twelve on Saturday. That gives you two days to talk to your dad and whoever. If we do this, we gotta do it right.'

As soon as the boys left, all the Fitzgeralds made their way to the living room to find out what the visit was all about, and Alem told them. Mrs Fitzgerald and Ruth both agreed that it was a great idea and they encouraged him to go ahead, but Mr Fitzgerald wasn't sure. He felt that if the political boat was rocked, the powers that be might make life even more difficult for Alem. After some gentle persuasion from Mrs Fitzgerald he conceded that it could be a good thing if Alem's father agreed.

Alem had the feeling that his father might not like the idea of a public campaign, so he was prepared, and the next day after school he made his way directly to the hotel to speak to him. He was right, his father was completely against the idea.

'No!' he shouted. 'We are in enough trouble as it is. We should wait for your appeal to be heard and we certainly should not be getting involved in the politics of this country. What we should be doing is being as peaceful as possible and making no fuss. We must not draw attention to ourselves.'

When his father was speaking in such a way, Alem knew that it wasn't the right time for him to speak, but for the first time ever he felt he needed to challenge his father's point of view.

'But Father, who knows what will happen to us if we get sent back? We have a right to life, we have the right to be protected, and sometimes these judges and adjudicator people get it wrong. That judge doesn't know anything about Ethiopia or Eritrea. He didn't even know when our Christmas was. Who is he?'

'He is the law,' Mr Kelo shouted, 'and the law of the land must be respected.'

'So we must go home to live in fear,' Alem said quietly.

'We must go home – if we are told to – and how we live is not the issue for the judge. You heard what he said; we are together, now it's up to us.'

'It's not fair,' Alem said stubbornly.

'Never mind fair, we will stay quiet and appeal. If we lose the appeal, we must go, that's the law. Never mind fair!' his father shouted.

'But you said this country has compassionate people who know what it's like to need refuge, people who understand, that's what you said.'

'That's right, I said that.'

'Well, those are the kind of people who want to help us now. Look!' Alem quickly unzipped his bag and pulled out the newspaper cuttings that he had been keeping. He handed them to his father. 'There are also people who are not compassionate, people who don't care. They call us tramps, thieves and beggars, they want to clamp down on us, they want to make us live on boats and in prisons.'

Mr Kelo looked at the cuttings and read the headlines. 'This is politics, young man, we should not be getting involved in these things. This has nothing to do with us!' he shouted, throwing the cuttings on to the bed.

'Everything is politics, Father, you know this. We are here because of politics, the judge is there because of politics, and we are being sent home because of politics.'

Mr Kelo started to pace up and down the room, beads of sweat appearing on his forehead. 'We are not going to get involved in any campaign,' he said angrily. 'If we deserve justice, we will get justice.'

Recalling what Asher had recently said to him, Alem replied, 'There ain't no justice, just us.'

Mr Kelo suddenly stopped. He stamped his foot on the floor and said firmly, 'I want you to stop answering me back and have some respect! Since when have you learned to speak to adults like that?'

Alem pleaded with him. 'But Father, please don't get angry with me. On Saturday my friends will be having a meeting. Please come with me and hear what they have to say.'

Mr Kelo sat down on one of the pink chairs. He didn't answer Alem for a minute. 'Yes, OK I will go with you. I shall go and listen to what your friends have to say.'

On Friday afternoon outside the school gate Alem, Buck and Robert had an impromptu meeting. 'My father does not like the idea of a campaign,' said Alem. 'The Fitzgeralds said it was a good idea but my father just went on about the law of the land and not causing any trouble.'

'Don't tell me you can't come tomorrow?' Robert said in resignation.

'No,' Alem replied, 'I will be coming but I will be with my father. He wants to see what it's all about.'

'That's even better,' said Robert joyfully. 'We want your dad there, it's about him too.'

When Alem arrived home there was more bad news for him and he knew it as soon as he reached the house. He could see Mariam's old Volkswagen parked outside and when he entered the house he could tell from Mrs Fitzgerald's manner that something was wrong. He looked in the living room, where he saw Mariam sitting with Sheila. Alem walked right in and sat down.

'What's the matter?' he said bluntly.

Sheila spoke. 'The problem is, Alem, that you were placed in the care of the local authority because you did not have a guardian in this country. Now that you do have a guardian, we've been told that your care order is being removed and that you're no longer in our care.'

Alem smiled. 'So what? That's not important, is it? I mean, you've been very good to me and I think that you have really helped, and Mr and Mrs Fitzgerald said that they don't mind looking after me,' he said, looking towards Mrs Fitzgerald.

'It's not as simple as that,' Sheila continued. 'Mr and Mrs Fitzgerald are foster parents working for the Social Services. They are carers, in effect, and once the care order has been removed, they cannot legally foster or adopt you.'

Alem looked around the room slowly. He thought someone was playing a sick joke but he could see by the stony faces that no one was joking. 'So what happens to me now?'

'Well,' Sheila said, 'you have to return to the care of your father.'

Alem didn't know whether to feel good or bad about this. 'Does he know about this?'

'Yes, I've just come from there.'

'Where will we live?'

Sheila leaned back in the seat, preparing for Alem's reaction. 'You'll have to stay with him in the hotel.'

'What? You mean in that little room?' Alem shouted. 'Have you seen it?'

'Yes, I've seen it and it's not a nice place but it's all we can do for now.'

'Well, at least I'm with my father and I won't be far from here.'

'And let's face it,' Mrs Fitzgerald said, 'you can come here any time and do whatever you like – eat, use the computer.'

'Feed the fish,' Mr Fitzgerald added.

'I'll need to, I think,' Alem said, smiling. 'You want to see that hotel, Mrs Fitzgerald. You haven't seen the inside – it's a bit rough.'

Sheila told them that she was still the appointed social worker for Alem but now she was the social worker for his father as well. The care order was being revoked on Monday the twenty-first.

When Mariam and Sheila left, Mr and Mrs Fitzgerald had a talk with Alem. They all agreed that although the hotel wasn't the best place in the world, at least he would be with his father, and that the Fitzgeralds should be thought of as an extended family. When Ruth got home she was told and she took the news badly, but she let Alem know that she was his sister and she would be there when he needed her.

The next morning a solemn Mr Kelo turned up at the Fitzgerald home. Both families talked for a while about the move the next day, and then he left on foot with Alem and Ruth for the rehearsal cellar.

Alem rang the bell and Robert opened the door.

'This is Robert,' Alem said to his father.

Robert stretched forth his hand. 'Hello, Mr Kelo, we're glad you could come.'

Mr Kelo shook his hand.

'Follow me,' Robert said, 'we were just about to start the meeting.'

Alem could hear noises coming from the cellar but was very surprised by what awaited him. The cellar was packed with kids, some that he had never seen before and some familiar faces from school. As Alem and his father entered the room, they all stopped chattering and clapped. As the clapping died down, Robert made his way to the front of the cellar where the band's equipment was. He stood on a makeshift podium made from the reinforced shipping cases used for the instruments, and opened the meeting.

'All right, we are here today because we all want justice for our friend Alem. We have all agreed that we're willing to help out in any way we can to get him and his father to stay in this country for as long as he needs to.'

There were shouts of approval from the crowd. Robert continued.

'It is easy to understand that some people may think we're starting trouble, but any campaign that we start must be a peaceful one. We must be in control and have discipline, because we know that the trouble has already been started. All we want is fair treatment for our fellow human beings. Now this is the plan of action. We shall march to the town hall on Saturday 11th March to deliver a petition to our MP or one of her people. The week before that, on the fourth, we'll have a benefit gig at the school featuring none other than Pithead, our own local protest band. We need to let all the churches, mosques and temples know what's happening and we need to tell the local press.' He paused and looked around the room. 'We're ready and we're willing! But anything we do, we must do it with the consent of both Alem and Mr Kelo, all right. So before we go any further we need to know from you –' he looked towards Alem and his father – 'if we have your permission to campaign on your behalf.'

The whole room fell silent. Everyone looked at Alem; Alem looked at his father, then everyone looked at Alem's father. Mr Kelo gazed around at all the eager young faces, obviously raring to go, and he considered for a moment how they had given up their time to be there. He looked towards Robert and nodded his head.

Everyone in the room shouted, 'Yes!' Many jumped for joy as if their team had scored a winning goal. Robert took control of the situation; it was as if he had been watching proceedings in the House of Commons.

'Order, order! he shouted at the top of his voice. 'Now, any volunteers? We need as many volunteers as possible.'

Mr Kelo watched in amazement as kids volunteered to do various duties. Alem could tell that his father was fighting back the tears that had begun to form in his eyes. Ruth went forward and volunteered to take the job of press and public-relations person and when she returned she hugged Alem, who was holding back his own tears.

Slowly, the crowd dispersed. It was as if they had all gone on a mission, a young army of resistance working for a cause they all believed in. Before they left, Mr Kelo spoke to as many of them as he could, including Asher and Buck, and he thanked them all for what they were doing. Then Mr Kelo, Alem and Ruth made their way back to Meanly Road.

CHAPTER 21

~ The Freedom Dance ~

The view from the bedroom window was deceptive. The morning sun shone as if it was midsummer and there was not a cloud in the sky but it was still cold outside. Alem packed his belongings slowly. He had come to the house with all he had packed into one sports bag; now he had to be given a large suitcase by Mr Fitzgerald to carry his things. As he packed, Mrs Fitzgerald came into the room. Alem looked sad.

'Don't worry, Alem, you're not really going anywhere. And Alem, you must take a couple of books. Bring them back when you're done with them, but do take some.'

Ruth stuck her head round the door. 'Hey, Alem, leave your family picture on the computer for now. If you really don't want it to stay on, we can take it off later, but I reckon you should leave it for a while. You gonna be around.'

Alem nodded his head in agreement. Then he began to pick up all the books from the floor and place them back on the bookshelves. Mrs Fitzgerald left him to it. When the books were on the shelves he realised that he hadn't chosen anything to take with him, so he began to browse over the titles until something caught his eye. It was *An Encyclopaedia of the English Language*. Alem took it off the shelf and flicked through a few pages. It wasn't just a dictionary, it had whole sections on how the English language had evolved, the differences between spoken English and written English, and it would also explain the history of some individual words. Alem placed it in the sports bag before making his way downstairs, where the Fitzgeralds were waiting for him.

The taxi pulled up outside and sounded its horn. Alem shook Mr Fitzgerald's hand on the doorstep, hugged Ruth and said goodbye, and then hugged Mrs Fitzgerald. 'I don't know what all this emotional stuff is about! You and your father will be back here tomorrow for a meal.'

'And we have a campaign committee meeting here on Wednesday,' said Ruth.

Mrs Fitzgerald placed a folded ten-pound note into Alem's hand and said, 'Taxi fare – keep the change. Now you go, say hello to your father for us, and we'll see you round here at six tomorrow.'

At the other end of the journey, Alem was struggling to get up the stairs with his luggage.

'Let me help you,' came a voice from the bottom of

the stairs. Alem turned to find the young man who had previously directed him to his father's room when he first came to visit him and whom he had last seen in the supermarket.

'Thanks,' Alem replied. 'If you take this bag, then I can carry the big one on my own. Carrying them both together is what I find difficult.'

When they reached the top of the stairs, the man began to question Alem.

'What is your name?'

'Alem, Alem Kelo.'

'Where do you come from?'

'Africa.'

'Let me guess where in Africa – Somalia?'

'No, close.'

'Sudan.'

'No.'

'Where then?'

'I come from Ethiopia and Eritrea.'

'I knew it was somewhere around there. This place has people from everywhere. There are a few Somalis and there was an Ethiopian family but they have gone now.'

Alem now began to question the man. 'What's your name?'

'My name is Abbas Noor and I am Palestinian.'

Alem began to think. 'I can't remember now, where is Palestine?'

'That is the problem. Palestine has been taken off the map.'

Alem was tempted to ask more questions about this country that sounded so familiar but wasn't on the map. However, he decided to pursue another line of questioning just in case he risked upsetting him. 'So how long have you been here?'

'I've been in the hotel for one year and before that we were in another place, it was worse than this.'

'What?' Alem couldn't believe what he was hearing. 'You mean there are places called hotels that are worse than this?'

'Listen, you see lots of them all over London. Even on this road there are a few hotels, yes?'

'Yes.'

'Well, this is the best one around here.'

'Honest?'

'I am serious, you should see some of the others. And I tell you something else. If you take some money and go into any of these hotels to rent a room, you will find that you will never get a room, they won't give you one, and most of them won't even have a reception.'

Alem thought about his first visit to the hotel and how he had looked for a reception desk but couldn't find one. He remembered never even seeing anyone who looked as if they were in charge. 'Why is that?' he asked. 'Why no reception? Why no rooms for hire?'

'Because they only want business from the Social Security. Money paid straight into their bank accounts. So they only take refugees and homeless people who the council send – regular money, you see.'

Mr Kelo heard them talking and came out to see who it was. 'Oh, it's you, Alem. Come on in and bring your friend.' He reached out and took the large suitcase.

'I must go – but I'll see you again. So you live here now?' Abbas asked, pointing into the room.

'Yes.'

'OK. Goodbye, sir,' he said to Mr Kelo. 'See you,' he said to Alem. 'What's your name again?'

'Alem.'

'Alem,' he repeated.

As soon as Alem entered the room he noticed that another piece of furniture had been added. A single bed made up with clean sheets, a duvet and a small flat pillow.

Mr Kelo saw that it had caught Alem's eye. 'Sheila had it delivered this morning,' he said. 'It's good to have friends in high places.'

The room was very different from the one Alem had just left, and everything about it made his skin crawl, but he thought that if his father could endure it, he should endure it with him. He had to share the wardrobe with his father's clothes, which were already sharing the wardrobe with the food. Alem now had nowhere but the floor to put his personal belongings and there was very little space in the room to move around. Later in the evening when no one was using the kitchen, they went down and cooked boiled potatoes and tinned mincemeat. Then Alem did some homework and Mr Kelo listened to the news on the radio until late into the night.

In the morning the cold and the sound of heavy traffic woke Alem. He blew into the air and watched his breath turn white. Then he put his head under the duvet and curled up tightly into a ball, hoping that he would quickly get warm, but it wasn't working so he got out of bed and prepared himself for school. School was now a bus ride away but he made sure that he arrived early.

After school he met up with his father at the Fitzgeralds' house, where they had a meal as planned.

The next day after school Alem was back at Meanly Road again, this time for the first campaign meeting. It was held in his old room, which had now been transformed into the co-ordination office of the campaign. The computer had been left on so that the Kelo family watched over them.

Alem had come from school with Robert and Buck,

and then Ruth arrived from work. Soon afterwards Asher and other volunteers turned up, including one girl that Alem had not seen before.

Asher introduced her to Alem. 'Hey, Alem,' he said, guiding her between them, 'this is Tibra. She's cool, man, from Ethiopia, a true Ethiopian princess.'

Alem shook her hand. 'Hello, pleased to meet you.'

She looked Ethiopian but Alem was shocked by her accent, which was completely east London with not a trace of African.

'I heard what was going down and I thought I gotta do something to help you.'

'Thank you. Where in Ethiopia do you come from?'

'My family come from Addis but I was born here. Never see Ethiopia in me life. Well, only on telly, like, and then we only see the bad bits.'

By now the room had nine people in it, which made it seem very crowded. Robert called the meeting to order and began the proceedings.

'Now, first of all I have to report that we have hired the school hall for the benefit gig. Now we need to get the posters designed and made up.'

Asher spoke. 'No problem. I'll deal with that, my friend works in a print shop. I'll arrange something with him. He's great at design as well.'

'Good,' Robert continued. 'Now what about the petition?'

'I'm doing that,' said a boy standing by the door.

Alem didn't recognise him. He whispered to Buck, 'Who's that?'

'That's Ajay Kumar, Mrs Kumar's son. Well-educated geezer, both parents are teachers, innit?'

'This is the wording,' Ajay continued. He began to read from a piece of paper. 'We, the undersigned, protest in the strongest terms against the planned deportation of Alem and Mr Kelo. As British subjects we believe that it is our duty to offer them protection until it is completely safe for them to return to their homeland. Furthermore we demand that our elected government set up an inquiry to look into the general treatment of refugees and asylum seekers.'

Ajay stopped and looked at Robert. 'If that's OK I'll get these photocopied tomorrow.'

'Does anyone object to that wording?' Robert asked. Everyone shook their heads. 'All right, get them photocopied, and Ruth,' he said, looking in her direction, 'what do you have for us?'

Ruth stepped into the middle of the room. 'Today I spoke to the *Newham Echo*. They said that they'd like to do a piece on Alem. They said they can't campaign on our behalf but they could do a kind of human-interest story. I've also been in touch with *Newstalk South East*, the TV programme. They said they'd cover both the march and the gig – if there are no major disasters in London when they're on. And I've

253

also been on the phone to the local MP, who promised to take the petition on the eleventh and deliver it to Number Ten Downing Street.'

Ruth sat down and Robert thanked her. Some other duties were delegated, including the job of planning the route of the march and notifying the police, which was shared between Tibra and Robert.

Then Robert made his final speech. 'Don't forget now, we don't have much time. We really need to get moving. Get petitions any time after tomorrow from Ajay in school or from Ruth here after five o'clock, and get as many signatures as you can. Get them from your friends, your neighbours, shopkeepers, your parents, even your local policeman. Don't stop getting them until those forms are full. Our next meeting will be here on the twenty-eighth at five. Hopefully by then we should be making some progress.'

After the meeting, when people were making their way out, Alem managed to get Ruth and Robert together. 'What can I do?' he said. 'I haven't got a job.'

'Don't worry,' replied Robert. 'We're doing this for you. You and your father have other things to get on with.'

'OK,' Alem said, now turning to Ruth. 'But what about your parents? We can't keep using the house as a meeting place.'

Ruth went up to him and put her arms around his

shoulders. 'You worry too much. Mum and Dad said it's fine. They told us to use it and they said they'll do anything to help, but only when asked. They want us to run this campaign ourselves. Adults must be accompanied by radical youths.'

Many of the activists were seeing each other at school, and Alem went to visit Asher at his flat and to see Pithead rehearse during that week.

At the next meeting it was obvious that all the jobs were being done; sheets of signed petitions were already being handed in, posters had been put up on the streets and the route of the march had been agreed.

Early on Saturday evening Alem and his father made their way to the school by bus. Inside the hall records were already playing and the hall was half full. The event was attracting a diverse range of people; many of Alem's fellow students were there, some of their parents, some teachers, more kids that looked like clones of Buck and many very familiar faces. Mariam, Sheila, Pamela and Alem couldn't believe their eyes when they saw Mr and Mrs Fitzgerald paying the going rate at the door before coming into the hall.

Soon the hall was packed and Robert appeared on stage. He took hold of the microphone and began to speak. 'I would like to thank you all for coming here tonight to support this cause. We will not give up this struggle because we are strong and I think we are getting stronger every day. Before we begin the entertainment tonight, I just want to remind you all of the march next week. We will be leaving Great Milford School on Saturday 11th March at eleven a.m., and from there we will be marching via a pre-planned route to Stratford Town Hall, where I shall be handing in a petition to Mrs Leonie Ranks MP. It is very important that we get as many people as possible on that march so please come, bring your friends and make sure that you have strong voices. Tonight we have a great local band to play for you. But before the band we have a local poet who is going to share his work with us, so please give a big welcome to Asher Obadiah.'

Robert walked off stage as the crowd began to clap, shout and whistle. Alem did a double-take when he realised that it was his friend Asher who was now standing on the stage. Wearing a West African gown and a red, yellow and green headband around his dreadlocks, Asher stood and delivered five poems, one after the other. The crowd applauded after each one. When he was about to do the final one, he dedicated it to Alem and Mr Kelo and all those who were fleeing from persecution.

When Asher left the stage, Robert reappeared. This time he was much quicker. 'And now for the main act of the night, the band of the future with their own home-grown indie sound – please welcome Pithead.

The band came on and started to play. Buck and the other band members seemed to have made no attempt to dress up, and Buck's style of singing still sounded like moaning to Alem.

Mr Kelo couldn't believe what he was hearing or seeing. He had always known music as a form of cele-bration. Even the music he had heard at funerals was a celebration of the life of the deceased, but these guys sounded as if they were in mourning. Everyone started dancing, and the people dancing looked as if they were enjoying the music more than the band members were. Mr Kelo raised his eyebrows at Alem. In the middle of the hall Mr and Mrs Fitzgerald were dancing completely out of time, looking out of place but having the time of their lives. Teachers danced like vicars at weddings, and students tried to dance as far away from the teachers as possible.

Buck introduced each song.

'This one's called, "Who Are the Living?"'

'This one's called, "She Took My Coat".'

'This one's called, "I Believe in Acne",' and so on.

At the end of the night Robert got back on stage and thanked everyone for coming. He reminded them of the march, then without warning he called Alem on stage to say 'a few words'.

Alem was taken aback; he didn't expect it and he had nothing prepared. His father nodded his head in the direction of the stage and Alem began to make his way slowly. He was so nervous that when he lightly touched the microphone, he could see his hand shaking; he had to grip it tightly in order to stop the shaking.

'I don't know what to say. I just want you to know that we are so happy that you are helping us and we hope one day to repay you for your kindness. Maybe one day there will be peace in my homeland and I can invite you all back for a big party.'

Everyone laughed and clapped their hands.

'Thank you very much, that's all I can say for now.'

As Alem left the stage, Robert darted back and quickly uttered a few more words. 'Before you go I just want to say that tonight we have raised seven hundred and thirty-five pounds, eighty-five pence.' There was another round of applause. 'And this money will go towards promoting the campaign and for expenses for Alem and his father if they need it. Thank you, and see you on Saturday!'

CHAPTER 22

~ The Word on the Streets ~

The next week flew past. Alem was quietly excited as he watched all his young activists organising the rally. Now posters could be seen all over the streets of Newham and neighbouring boroughs. On Wednesday night Alem and Mr Kelo were invited to St Emmanuel Parish Church, where the Newham Echo interviewed and photographed them for the weekend edition. The priest and the users of the community centre expressed their support for them.

On Saturday morning the sun shone. Alem noticed that the cold was less biting. He and his father took a bus to the school. They had simply not prepared themselves for what they saw. Hundreds of people had gathered there, many of them carrying banners with slogans:

'Alem Kelo must stay.'

'Home, sweet home.'

'Refugees need homes too.'

'There are no illegal immigrants, only illegal governments.'

Mr Kelo grabbed Alem's hand. 'Look at all these people,' he said. 'They are all here for us! Where did they come from?' He was astounded by the range of people: young, old, Black, Asian, White, men in suits, girls in suits, new-age hippies, punks, Rastas and Buck lookalikes.

'Look, Father,' Alem said, pointing ahead, 'there's Abbas.' And there he was carrying a banner: 'Refugees are human, let us live.'

Then Alem felt a tap on his shoulder; he turned around to find an excited, smiling boy. Alem hesitated a little; he did not recognise the boy who was reaching out to shake his hand. His face was quite badly scarred.

'Hi, Alem,' the boy said, shaking Alem's hand enthusiastically. 'My name's Martin. I made these for the campaign. What do you think of them?' He handed a badge to Alem. It read, 'Refugees make great lovers.'

Alem smiled and said, 'Very good.' He turned to show it to his father. Mr Kelo shook his head and smiled in amusement.

'Wear it,' Martin said. 'Put it on, man.'

Alem looked towards his father for approval. His father nodded. 'Go ahead.'

Alem pinned it on his jacket. 'I must thank you for making them, it's a great idea.'

'No problem, mate,' Martin said, taking another

one out of his pocket and handing it to Mr Kelo. 'Here's one for you, Mr Kelo.'

'It's OK,' Mr Kelo replied, 'they don't look very good on me.'

Martin laughed and said, 'I just want to say good luck to you. I support you all the way – don't let them get you down, stay strong! I must go and shift some badges – see you.' He turned and disappeared into the crowd as quickly as he had appeared.

Ruth spotted Alem and Mr Kelo making their way through the crowd, so she waded in to rescue them and take them to what was to become the front of the procession. This was where most of his friends were; Buck, Mr and Mrs Fitzgerald, Asher, Mrs Kumar – the head of his year – and her son Ajay, as well as some other teachers, and they were all being watched by the police.

Robert appeared with a megaphone. 'How you going, Alem? What a turnout! Good, hey?'

'It's amazing,' Alem replied.

'Hello, Mr Kelo.'

'Hello, Robert. You have done such a great job.'

'We haven't finished yet, Mr Kelo. There's this rock song, right, it's a bit dull, a bit like that music you heard last week. Anyway that song says it ain't over till it's over. And that's it, Mr Kelo: it ain't over till it's over.'

'Very good,' said Mr Kelo.

Alem heard a whisper over his shoulder. 'Tena-yestelen.' He had not heard any Amharic for a long time. He looked around quickly; it was Tibra.

'Tena-yestelen,' Alem replied.

His father heard Amharic being spoken and turned to see them both.

'Tena-yestelen, Mr Kelo,' Tibra said.

'Tena-yestelen,' Mr Kelo replied.

'Father, this is Tibra,' Alem said quickly. 'As you can hear she's from Ethiopia – well, she was born here.'

'So you speak Amharic?' Mr Kelo asked.

'No,' she replied. 'I just know how to say hello, goodbye, not much else. My family came here when there was all that fighting in 1974, a long time before I was born.'

Just then Robert began to speak with the loud-hailer. 'Now we shall begin our march. Please try and keep in line! Be as loud as you can but be orderly. If anyone feels ill, please let one of the stewards know as soon as possible. And whatever you do, remember to be well-mannered to the pedestrians and car drivers. OK, here we go!'

Robert turned and began to lead with Alem and his father at his side. Alem's closest friends were behind them, followed by the rest of the marchers. Robert started chanting into his megaphone and the crowd followed him.

'Don't make the Kelos go – no, no, no, no.'

'Don't make the Kelos go – no, no, no, no.'

And 'What do we want?'

'Justice for the Kelos?'

'When do we want it?'

'Now!'

And 'Solidarity, solidarity, every refugee needs solidarity.'

People clapped as they chanted and a few people played small drums and cymbals. Martin was weaving in and out of the crowd, distributing his badges. There was a carnival atmosphere with many cars sounding their horns in support, but as the front of the march reached the junction of Romford Road and Shrewsbury Road, a large people carrier full of people slowed down.

The windows of the van were rolled down and six men in their early twenties began to shout, 'Go home!' 'Go and march in your own country!' 'Pakis . . .'

One of them spat in the direction of the demonstration. Some demonstrators broke away and began throwing stones at the van. The men in the van started throwing stones back and for a moment there was a mini riot. Alem and his father were surrounded by their supporters. They were both frightened and saddened that violence had broken out. A group of police officers moved in on foot to try to part the warring sides, but it wasn't until the sound of sirens could be heard that the men jumped back into their van and drove off. The police van followed behind them and the demonstrators watched the police stop them about half a mile up the road. The demonstrators reassembled and the march continued. Robert began leading the chants and soon got back the carnival spirit. As they crossed Green Street, an Indian restaurant started to hand out free vegetable samosas to those that wanted them.

Mrs Kumar smiled at Alem. 'That's my sister's business.'

From the school to the town hall it took just over two hours but the conversations, the singing and the chanting meant that it felt much shorter. Outside the town hall the people gathered on the pavement on both sides of the road to hear the speeches. As the Fitzgeralds, Robert, Mariam, Alem and his father stood on the steps of the town hall, Robert lifted the megaphone and began his speech.

'Thank you for coming here today. As you know, we have organised this march because we want to send a message to the people who make the rules, the politicians. This march has been organised to let these people know that Alem Kelo and his father deserve the right to live without fear. Now I'm not a very good speaker, so what I'm going to do now is hand you over to Mariam Desta from the Refugee Council.'

There was clapping and whistleblowing as Mariam took the megaphone. 'Girls and boys, ladies and gentlemen! I have been on many demonstrations in my time working for the Refugee Council. Every time people take to the streets it is important, but I have to say that this is a very special demonstration. Special because it is in support of two very special people, and special because it has been organised by some other very special people. The banner, the route, the publicity, the fundraising, the petition, everything about this demonstration has been organised by Alem's friends. This march is truly an example of youth power. It is time that the voice of the youth be heard on this matter, because the youth matter!'

There was a loud round of applause, with shouts and whistles.

'I have known Alem since he first came to this country,' Mariam continued, 'and he is one of the most conscientious, hard-working, intelligent people that I've ever met, and I've met a lot of people, young and old. He has come through great hardship and he is a great survivor. But as you all know, we have reached a crucial point. A judge has said that he must return to his persecution. A judge who has never sat down and talked to Alem about his fears and dreams is sending him back to a nightmare to live in danger.

We must not let that happen! We at the Refugee Council are supporting Alem and his father because we know what it is like to live in fear of your life. We work every day with people who are persecuted because of their political beliefs, their race, their gender and even their language, and we will never stand aside and watch them suffer. We support the Kelos and I just want to thank you for supporting them too.'

Robert took the megaphone from Mariam as she stepped aside, and he began to speak when the applause had died down. 'Now, I must say that I haven't warned him that I'm going to do this, and I hope that he forgives me, but I would like to ask Alem to say a few words.'

Alem shook his head vigorously. He didn't want to stand in front of so many people. He looked at the large crowd and his stomach churned. He looked at his father, who shrugged his shoulders as if to say, 'It's up to you, don't ask me.' He looked towards Ruth, who just smiled, and Mr Fitzgerald put a thumb up to him. But still he didn't want to face the crowd until the crowd started chanting, 'Alem, Alem, Alem, Alem,' and the longer he left it, the louder they got.

Alem moved towards Robert and took the megaphone. He looked out over the sea of people and took a deep breath.

'My name is Alem Kelo and I really can't understand why I am here. You see, in my homeland they are fighting over a border, a border that is mainly dust and rocks. I really cannot understand why these people are fighting over this border. If there is to be any fighting, we should be having a nonviolent fight to get rid of borders.'

The crowd erupted in cheers.

'I haven't come to England to become a problem. I didn't leave the land that I love so much to be so cold.'

The crowd laughed.

'But what can I do? At the moment they are fighting and not talking. If they ever start talking, they may arrange a time to negotiate. If they do ever negotiate, they may draw up a peace treaty. If they ever manage to draw up a peace treaty, they will have to agree on it, and if they ever agree on it, they may sign it. But it is only a peace treaty, a peace deal, a piece of paper. What we really want is a culture of peace! We must raise a new generation of peacemakers.'

The crowd erupted again.

'I don't know what else to say because I had not planned to make a speech. But I want to thank you from the bottom of my heart for your support. Since I have been in this country I have made some very good friends, and now I look at all of you and I feel like you are all my friends.'

The crowd clapped and shouted, 'Alem, Alem, Alem!'

'You make me feel so good!' There was more laughter. 'Yes, my name is Alem. In my language Alem means "world". I would love to see the day when there are no more refugees in the world and the world can live in peace. Then when I would come to England I would come to see my friends and instead of demonstrating we would be celebrating.' He paused for thought. 'But I would come in the summer when it's warm.'

There was more loud laughter and applause. Alem let the crowd settle down. 'Before I go I have a request.'

Suddenly there was silence as they waited to hear what he was in need of.

'I would like one last thing: I would like my father to come up here and introduce himself to you.'

The crowd cheered. Alem, Robert and the other people on the steps all gestured to Mr Kelo to step forward. Mr Kelo knew from the noise of the crowd that it would be very difficult for him to decline. As he took the megaphone from Alem, they hugged each other to the delight of the crowd.

'I want to thank each one of you for coming today. It really does mean so much to us. I love my country, so I will always try to work for peace there, but every day I and my son Alem have to live with the knowledge that right now our country is at war with itself. Mrs Kelo – my wife, his mother – was killed there.

Her life was taken by people who are really not concerned about the wellbeing of our country. She was concerned, so now she is our inspiration, she is the symbol of what is possible, because she believed that human beings are capable of enormous love when we put our hearts together. And if she were here today, each one of you would know that she represents unity and that's what we must strive for. And I have one last message; this message is for the Eritreans and Ethiopians that are killing each other. Stop it! War is not the answer, only love will conquer. Stop fighting and let us live!'

The crowd went absolutely wild. The Fitzgeralds, Alem, Mariam and Robert joined hands across the stage and held them high.

Robert whispered to the doorman of the town hall, who then went inside. Mr Kelo handed Robert the megaphone and Robert began to speak. 'I have here –' he waved in the air many pieces of paper tied together with a ribbon – 'six thousand signatures that have been collected in less than three weeks, which I am now going to present to Mrs Leonie Ranks MP.'

Mrs Ranks came out from the town hall with the doorman standing at her side. Robert's words were now addressing Mrs Ranks but he was still using the megaphone so that the crowd could hear.

'Mrs Ranks, as you can see by the size of this demonstration and those six thousand signatures, there are many people who are not happy with the way refugees are treated. We are the young people who are growing up in this country and we demand better treatment for refugees, you know, more compassion. I have looked at your family history and I see that your family came here as refugees. This country of ours was once empty and barren so in some ways we are all refugees. So please take this to the Prime Minister and let him know how we feel.'

The crowd erupted again and Mrs Leonie Ranks MP went back into the building without saying a word. Robert raised the megaphone to his mouth one last time and shouted, 'Go home now, people, and prepare for a revolution!'

The crowd clapped and began to disperse.

CHAPTER 23

~ This is War Too ~

Alem and his father made a conscious decision to take it easy the next day. For most of the morning they stayed in the hotel, but late in the afternoon Mr Kelo decided that he wanted to do some shopping.

As they were going downstairs, they heard a voice shout out, 'Hello, my friend!'

It was Abbas, who then started to chant, 'Alem, Alem, Alem!' He was soon joined by what looked to Alem like Abbas's smaller brother and two other African children whose little voices began to accompany Abbas. 'Alem, Alem, Alem!'

Alem and Mr Kelo smiled.

'Hey, Alem,' Abbas shouted down the stairs, 'much respect! You're a freedom fighter!'

They didn't spend very long at the supermarket; all they put in their basket was a small amount of vegetables, more tinned meat and a packet of biscuits. As they were queuing for the cashier, Alem noticed that other checkouts were less busy.

'Father, look at those other counters! Why are we waiting in this long queue? Let's go to one of them.'

Mr Kelo's eyes dropped as he realised that Alem didn't know the deal. 'We can't,' he said, 'we don't have any money.'

'So what are you paying with?'

Mr Kelo took out his wallet and pulled out what looked like tickets. 'These, I have to pay with these. These are vouchers; look up there.'

He pointed to a sign above the counter where they were waiting. It read, 'Food vouchers only.'

'What is this all about?' Alem asked.

'These vouchers are for asylum seekers. We cannot buy clothes with them, we cannot get any change from our shopping with them, and we cannot use them at any other counter.'

Then Alem realised that he was waiting in the same place where he had seen Abbas three weeks ago and that Abbas may have not responded to him because he was feeling humiliated. The queue was long and full of exactly the same kind of people Alem had seen outside the courtrooms, Asians, Africans, Romanians and Kosovans, all waiting with their heads hanging down, looking humiliated. Meanwhile many other cashiers were sitting filing their nails or combing their hair, waiting for customers. Other shoppers just seemed to be a lot happier and some looked over to the 'Vouchers only' queue as if the customers

272

there were exhibition pieces.

Alem could also see the humiliation on his father's face but as for himself he felt angry; he didn't want to show it but he felt really angry. His father was a qualified person who had been in a good job and always proud to have earned every penny he had, but now he had been reduced to what amounted to living off aid. As Alem looked up and down the queue, he wondered how many people there were in the same position. Which of the men and women were doctors, lawyers, nurses or mathematicians? Could he be standing next to one of Bosnia's most promising architects, or an Iranian airline pilot? His father saw him silently shake his head in disgust as they shuffled down the line.

When Alem arrived at school the next day, he received a hero's welcome. Students he had never noticed before said hello to him. In the playground Robert came rushing up to him. 'Did you see us on the telly?'

'What?' Alem said. 'Slow down.'

'Did you see us on *Newstalk South East* on the television?'

'No,' Alem replied, 'we don't have a television, only a radio.'

'Well, did you hear us on the radio? They used part of your speech.'

'No.' Alem was surprised. 'They used my speech?'

'Yes, well, part of it.'

'What did it sound like?'

'It sounded wicked, guy. You were like Martin Luther King or some freedom fighter.'

The school assembly proceedings started as normal until the headmaster stopped talking about students running in the corridors and started talking about Saturday.

'On Saturday there was a large event which many of you took part in and some of you may have seen on television. That event was organised by many pupils from this school and I think that it was a very significant event. As the headmaster of this school it is not my job to get involved in your politics, but I do think that it is very good that so many of you here felt so strongly about an issue that you were willing to take to the streets for it. When I saw the size of the demonstration and the publicity it generated, I thought of how much you kids can do when you really want to achieve something and the way you worked together. I won't mention any names but I know that many of you worked hard to make that demonstration a success.

'I do feel as if what I should be doing this morning is giving you all a Positive School Certificate, but I fear some other headmaster in some other school might think me arrogant. What I would like to do, in a way on behalf of you all, is give the Positive Pupil Certificate to one very special boy, Alem Kelo. Not only has Alem had to deal with coming very suddenly to a new country and a new school but he has also had to deal with family tragedies that anyone would find hard to endure. When times were hard and many of us would have stayed at home, Alem came to school. He values education. Within a very short period of time he has excelled in the classroom, his interest in literature and language is passionate, his quest for knowledge is relentless, and I have never met anyone who has had a bad word to say about his behaviour and attitude. He is a hard-working, strong, intelligent student who must be seen as an example to us all, and I now ask him to step up here and collect his Positive Pupil Certificate.'

The students and teachers clapped. For a moment Alem just couldn't move from his seat. Cheers were added to the claps and Alem could hear someone say, 'Go on, Alem.'

Alem stood up and made his way on stage. As the clapping died down, the headmaster handed Alem the certificate and spoke again. 'Well done to all of you for standing up for your beliefs! And well done, Alem, for showing such great character!'

Alem held the award high in the air and the applause started again. It didn't finish until he was back in his seat, totally engrossed in reading the wording on the certificate to himself.

The moment school was over, Alem headed to Meanly Road to see the Fitzgeralds. At the door Mrs Fitzgerald hugged and kissed him as she praised him. She took the certificate from him and ran into the living room to show it to Mr Fitzgerald, who was reading a newspaper.

'Alem, we are so proud of you,' Mrs Fitzgerald said as she admired the certificate in its frame. 'You have done so well!'

Alem sat down and shook his head. 'That's what I don't understand, Mrs Fitzgerald – what have I done so well? I haven't done anything. Ruth has done more than me, Robert has done more than me, you have done more than me.'

'Nonsense,' said Mrs Fitzgerald, dismissing Alem's comments, 'you've done plenty.'

'Plenty of what? I haven't organised a demonstration; I haven't given anyone a home. I'm not a teacher, I haven't taught anybody anything.'

'That's where you're wrong,' said Mr Fitzgerald.

'Very wrong,' said Mrs Fitzgerald. 'You have shown courage. Look how well you're doing in school, you're like a role model. Yes, that's right, a role model. Someone that people look up to – even we look up to you.'

'That's right,' Mr Fitzgerald said, throwing his

newspaper on the table. 'Kids give in too easy nowa-days, they're what I call the impatient generation, but not you, you don't give in.'

'And that's why people respect you,' Mrs Fitzgerald filled in. 'Now, do you want some cola?'

Alem stood up. 'No, thank you, I must go home. My father is waiting for me.'

When Alem arrived at the hotel he found that the door to their room was locked and his father was nowhere to be seen. On the floor there was a letter addressed to his father. He picked it up and sat on the top stair, holding the letter and the certificate, waiting for his father to arrive. But he just waited and waited and after an hour he decided that he had to make some enquiries. He went to the first floor and knocked on Abbas's door.

His mother answered. 'You want Abbas?' she said in broken English.

'Yes, please,' replied Alem. 'Is he here?'

'Yes,' she said, 'but you must wait one minute, he is praying. So you are Alem?'

'Yes.'

'You are from Africa?'

'Yes.'

'I see you on television. You are revolution man, yes?'

'No, not really. I am just a normal boy.'

'No, you revolution man. Everybody say you are like Nelson Mandela.'

The thought of being compared to Nelson Mandela panicked Alem. 'No, I'm not like Nelson Mandela! I'm not revolution man.'

'So what you on television for?' Her expression became very serious.

'Nothing. I want . . . freedom, that's all – freedom and justice.'

Suddenly her expression changed to a smile but it was the smile of a beggar. She held out her hand. 'Can you get freedom and justice for me? On the television you must talk about me too.'

'All right, Mum,' said Abbas, interrupting the conversation from inside the room. 'I'm here now.'

She thanked him, turned and walked away. Abbas took her place at the door. 'How are you?'

'I'm OK,' said Alem, 'but I have a little problem.'

'What?'

'It's just my father. He's gone out somewhere and the room is locked so I can't get in.'

Abbas began to put on his shoes that were behind the door. 'No problem. You want to get into your room?'

'Yes.'

'I will get you into your room, easy.'

'How?'

'You watch me,' he said as he went up the stairs

ahead of Alem.

Outside the door Alem looked on in amazement as Abbas took a phone card, inserted it in the area of the lock and moved it about a little, causing the door to open, all in less than thirty seconds.

'How did you do that?' he said, staring into the room.

'It's easy. Every room is the same. You must never leave valuables in these rooms. Everyone knows how to get in them.'

'Have you seen my father today?' Alem asked.

'Yes, I saw him going out. Actually I spoke to him.'

'What did he say?'

'Nothing much. We just spoke a little about the demonstration and he was saying how proud he was of you, and that was it really.'

'About what time was that?'

'It was just after two o'clock. I know because I had just finished praying.'

'Thanks,' said Alem.

'Hey, what's that you have there?' Abbas asked, looking down at the frame Alem was holding closely to his chest.

'I was given a certificate today at school. It's nothing really.'

'OK. I'll see you later,' Abbas said heading downstairs.

'Yes, later,' Alem shouted.

Alem entered the room and closed the door behind him. He looked around the room for the best place to put his certificate. He wanted a place where his father could easily spot it as he walked in. No nails and hammer meant that it couldn't be hung up, so, knowing that his father would turn the radio on when he came in, he leaned it against the radio. Once he was happy that the certificate was in the best place, he began to browse through his dictionary.

Soon Alem heard footsteps coming up the stairs. His first instinct was to look towards the certificate to make sure that it was still standing. He sat up at the end of the bed as if waiting to be inspected, but then he realised that the footsteps might not be his father's. He could hear a conversation so he knew this was more than one person. However, they approached the door and there was a light knock. Alem went and opened the door to find Sheila and Mariam, but they were accompanied by a man that he had never seen before.

'Can we come in, please, Alem?' Sheila asked.

'Sorry, of course,' Alem said, realising that he had been staring at them for some length of time.

Sheila and Mariam went into the room, leaving the man loitering at the top of the stairs.

'Alem,' said Sheila, 'please sit down. You must prepare yourself. We have some very bad news.'

Alem sat on one of the chairs. He could see the

seriousness on everyone's faces. 'What's the matter?' he said anxiously. 'What's wrong? Who's that man?'

Mariam dropped her head as if trying to avoid Alem's eyes. Sheila continued, 'Alem, something terrible has happened. This afternoon there was an incident and your father was shot.'

Alem went numb. Everything and everybody in the room went out of focus as he tried to take in what had been said. 'No,' he moaned quietly. Then he shouted loudly, 'No! He is only missing, he will be back soon.' Alem shook his head to clear his vision and his mind. He looked at Mariam. 'Where is he? Mariam, where is my father?'

'It's very hard, Alem, but try to be calm,' Mariam said.

He looked back at Sheila. 'Who is that man out there?'

'A police officer,' Sheila said softly.

'My father has been shot.' Alem grabbed his jacket. 'Take me to him!'

'Try to calm down,' said Mariam.

'How do you expect me to calm down – he has been shot, is this really true?'

'I'm afraid it is true, Alem,' Sheila said.

Alem put his jacket on. 'And where is he now? Take me to him,' he said forcefully. 'I want to see him now. Please take me to the hospital now.'

'Please, Alem, sit down,' Sheila coaxed him gently.

'I need to talk to you some more.'

'I want to see my father now,' he said angrily.

'Please, Alem, please sit down.'

Alem sat back down on his chair and Sheila pulled up the other chair and sat in front of him.

'I'm sorry, Alem, but your father has died.' Sheila bowed her head after she spoke. As Alem looked at the silent bowed heads he knew that this was real.

The silence was broken by Alem's crying. It started with a slight sniffle, slowly building up until there was an explosion of tears. Mariam went and stood behind him and put her hand on his shoulder. They let the crying die down naturally until he was just sniffling and trying to wipe away his tears with his sleeve.

As Sheila handed him a small packet of tissues, Alem tried to talk but talking was difficult, pushing words out of his mouth felt like hard work. 'Who killed my father? Where was he killed?'

'We don't know who did it,' Mariam replied. 'The killer got away. But it happened outside the office of EAST, in Tottenham, just as he was leaving.'

Sheila stood up. 'The police are trying to find out who did it. You must get some rest, Alem. Tonight you should go and stay at Meanly Road.'

'No,' Alem said firmly, 'I want to stay here.'

'You can't stay here on your own,' Mariam said, 'you really can't.'

'Come on,' Sheila said, 'let us take you. They know

what's happening and they asked you to stay with them.'

'I want to stay here,' Alem insisted.

'You can't,' said Sheila.

Alem thought for a while and then stood up. 'Do I have to take anything?'

'Not for now,' said Mariam, rubbing his back.

As they were leaving, Mariam was about to shut the door when Alem said, 'Hold on, don't shut the door.' She waited as he went back into the room and took the family photograph from the table. Then they left.

Alem and the Fitzgeralds stayed up together until three o'clock in the morning and even after retiring Alem didn't sleep until four. At times he tortured himself trying to imagine the painful and brutal ways that both his parents had died. He would run various scenarios through his mind, then shake his head when he couldn't take it any more. He wondered what the future held for him without them, and then he began to feel guilty for thinking about himself. When he did sleep, he slept very little, and he woke up before anyone else in the house.

Later in the morning Sheila came to the house. She took Alem back to the hotel, where the police were now searching the room. Alem disliked the intrusion.

'What are they doing here?' he asked Sheila.

'Well, they have to do these checks to see if there

are any clues that could help lead them to the killer.'

'But we have so little here.'

'Yes but it's their job. For now you should take what you need.'

Once again Alem was packing his suitcase. The policeman he had seen the night before began to speak to him. 'I'm sorry for having to bother you now but I just wanted to say . . .' He hesitated. 'Alum, is it?'

'It's Alem.'

'Al-em – I'm sorry, can I call you Alan or Al maybe?'

'No,' Alem replied firmly, 'my name is not Alan, it's Alem.'

'Yes, of course, excuse me,' he said tactfully. 'Well – we may have to interview you at some stage.'

'OK.'

'I know it's very difficult but if we leave all our inquiries too late it becomes harder to find the perpe-trators. We need to get things done soon, so we'll be in touch.'

Sheila handed him her business card. 'He will be staying with foster parents. That has my work and home number on it. I would appreciate it if you got directly in touch with me when you want to speak to him.'

'Of course,' he said. 'One more thing; we found this letter and we're a bit concerned about it.'

He held up a letter. Alem could see that it was the letter that he had picked up the day before.

'Why does it concern you so much?' Sheila asked.

'Well, we can see that it has come from the courts, it has the coat of arms on it and we just felt that it may be important. What I would like to suggest is that you open it now, so that if it is something important you can act on it straightaway, and we can see if there's anything that we can do to help.'

Sheila took the envelope from him and opened it. She read it to herself. Then she looked at Alem. 'It's about your appeal. It says that your appeal will be heard on 27th March, 2000.'

CHAPTER 24

~ The News ~

The Metropolitan Police are investigating the killing of a man in Tottenham, north London. The incident happened yesterday afternoon as the man was leaving a community centre in Lordship Lane. Police believe that the killing may have been politically motivated. The victim held both Ethiopian and Eritrean nationality and was involved in an organisation set up to try and bring the two warring communities together. A statement issued by the police said that, although the police do believe that the shooting was political, it may be very difficult to identify any single political group that would have a motive. The statement went on to say that the killing could have been done by an Eritrean or an Ethiopian group, or any other group opposed to peace and reconciliation in the disputed region.

On the Saturday edition of this programme we covered a demonstration in support of the man and his son, who were being denied refugee status by the Home Office. In that report we featured speeches by the father and son, who have earned the respect of many young people in the East End of London. Friends and supporters say the boy is devastated and that he has been offered counselling.

CHAPTER 25

~ Judgement Day ~

It was 27th March. The court was full of Alem's friends and supporters. Those that could not fit inside gathered outside, making what amounted to a demonstration. Outside they chanted and sang in support of Alem; inside they sat silently as the new adjudicator read the many papers in front of him.

The adjudicator looked up and spoke. 'I have given careful consideration to the background material placed before me. While I shall say that the previous ruling in this case was a valid one, I have to take into account the appalling tragedy that has fallen upon you. I do have the power to make extrastatuary recommendations and today I shall exercise that power. Due to the exceptional circumstances of this case, I shall be recommending to the Home Office that the previous judgement be overturned and that you are granted exceptional leave to remain. You are free to go.'

CHAPTER 26

~ The End? ~

On Tuesday 20th December, 2000, the Ethiopian government and the Eritrean government signed a peace treaty in Algeria.

CHAPTER 27

~ Let Me Speak ~

My name is Alem Kelo. I live with the Fitzgeralds, my foster family, at 202 Meanly Road, Manor Park, London. I have also lived in Ethiopia and Eritrea. I have spent a few nights in a hotel in Datchet, one night in a children's home in Reading, and for a short while I stayed in a hotel in Forest Gate, which was a bit rough. I have stayed in all these places in the last year. To be really honest I would prefer to live in Africa with my mother and my father but they have both been killed and there is war in my country. Things are very hard for me. Look at me, look at all the things that I am capable of, and think of all the things you could call me – a student, a lover of literature, a budding architect, a friend, a symbol of hope even, but what am I called? A refugee. Some people believe that I gave up my homeland and lost my parents in order to become a refugee; some people actually believe that I gave up thirteen months of sunshine to live in the cold and to be called a scrounger. I didn't. Circumstances beyond my control brought me here, and all that I can do now is pick

290

myself up and try my best to make something out of what is left of my life. If good can come from bad, I'll make it. Fortunately, I have some good friends and a family that cares about me so I am not alone. I'm going to get some qualifications, a bike, and a girl-friend maybe, and if I'm able to, some time in the future I shall repay all that this country has given me. I am not a beggar, I am not bogus. My name is Alem Kelo.

This is not The End

Refugee Writes

Dear Mother,

I keep shedding tears,
Even in these my tender years
I don't have dreams
I have nightmares,
Dear Mother how I cry.

Dear Father,

How I really wish
That you could watch me learn English,
Each thought of you I now cherish,
How often can we die?

Dear Africa,

You must unite
And let your unity ignite
And then your people will shine bright,
Your greatness must be known.

Dear Britain,

I've found refuge here,
But all of us came from somewhere
And I can't simply disappear,
Compassion must be shown.

In the U. S., England, and elsewhere
around the world there are many
organizations that are offer help
and practical assistance to refugees
and asylum seekers.

Some of those organizations are:

Refugee Council
3 Bondway
London SW8 1SJ
UK
www.refugeecouncil.org.uk

U.S. Committee for Refugees
1717 Massachusetts Ave. NW
Suite 200
Washington, DC 20036
www.refugees.org

Immigration and Refugee Services of America
1717 Massachusetts Ave. NW
Suite 200
Washington, DC 20036
www.refugeesusa.org

American Refugee Committee International
430 Oak Grove Street, Suite 204
Minneapolis, MN 55403 USA
www.archq.org/global.shtml

International Rescue Committee
122 East 42nd Street
New York, New York 10168-1289
www.theirc.org

f a c e

b e n j a m i n   z e p h a n i a h

Witch Child

Celia Rees

'A powerful, absorbing and unusual novel' *The Bookseller*

old magic

marianne curley

a boy, a girl, a curse ... powerful chemistry!